"You're not naked," she said

Josh turned to find Holly standing in the doorway, wearing a short black satin robe. Thigh-high black stockings hugged her shapely legs. He started to whistle his appreciation, but once she stepped forward and touched him, everything faded in the soft press of her fingertips against his bare stomach.

"Here, let me help you with those." She gripped the zipper of his jeans and his breath caught. Metal hissed, the zipper eased and desire knotted in his gut.

Josh had always been the one to take the lead and do the undressing. The looking was the best part, or so he'd always thought. Until that moment.

Holly slipped her satiny fingers inside his BVDs and tugged them down. Then she stopped, her attention fixed on his crotch, and a strange mixture of emotion swirled through him. Half of him wanted to haul her into his arms and kiss her tenderly, while the other half wanted to bend her over and drive into her like a man possessed.

Josh did neither. It was Holly's recipe and she was doing the cooking.

For now.

Dear Reader,

My heroes have *always* been bad boys....

The McGraw brothers are the hunkiest bachelors in Romeo, Texas. They're rough and tough, wild and wicked, and they mean to stay that way.

Especially Josh McGraw.

After witnessing his parents' loveless marriage, Josh isn't in any hurry to commit to any woman. But when he meets gourmet dessert chef Holly Farraday and gets a taste of her prizewinning Ultimate Chocolate Orgasm, he finds himself craving more. Not that he's falling in love, mind you. It's all about sex.

As the newbie in town, Holly is eager to make friends and anxious to live up to her grandmother's legendary reputation as the town's resident sex expert. The problem? While Holly's got it going in the kitchen, she's not the least bit experienced when it comes to the bedroom. She needs Josh. Just for sex, mind you, nothing more.

Wrong!

I hope you enjoy reading about Holly and Josh's romantic adventures. Visit me online at www.kimberlyraye.com and let me know what you think!

Much love from deep in the heart,

Kimberly Raye

P.S. The heat wave continues next month in *Texas Fire* when wild, wicked Mason McGraw decides to give the town's most uptight woman a few lessons in how to really loosen up.

KIMBERLY RAYE
TEXAS FEVER

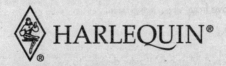

HARLEQUIN®

TORONTO • NEW YORK • LONDON
AMSTERDAM • PARIS • SYDNEY • HAMBURG
STOCKHOLM • ATHENS • TOKYO • MILAN • MADRID
PRAGUE • WARSAW • BUDAPEST • AUCKLAND

This book is dedicated to my editor, Brenda Chin,
for having faith in me and my ideas.
What would I do without you?

ISBN 0-373-79195-X

TEXAS FEVER

Copyright © 2005 by Kimberly Raye Groff.

www.eHarlequin.com

Printed in U.S.A.

1

HOLLY FARRADAY made it a rule never to pick up men in bars. But when she saw the cowboy standing near the pool table that occupied the far corner of the only saloon in Romeo, Texas, she couldn't help making an exception.

Cowboy, as in the real deal. There was no loud, blinding Western-cut snap shirt. No dark, stiff jeans. No polished ostrich cowboy boots or barely worn silver belly hat typical of the drugstore variety back in Houston.

Faded Wrangler jeans molded to his hips and thighs and accented long, sturdy legs that led to worn brown cowboy boots. An equally faded denim button-up shirt outlined his broad shoulders, the cuffs rolled up to reveal tanned forearms sprinkled with golden brown hair. A weathered straw Resistol, the front cocked down just a notch and the sides turned up, sat atop his head. Thick, dark hair curled down around his neck and brushed his collar. A rawhide leather choker clung to the tanned column of his throat. He had a strong jaw shadowed with stubble, a firm mouth and a strong nose.

But even more than his appearance, it was the way he carried himself that said he didn't just talk the talk when it came to the big *C*. He leaned against the far wall, so cocky and self-assured as he sipped an icy bottle of Coors Light and surveyed the game of eight ball being played in front of him. He oozed strength and an air of raw sensuality that attracted her on a deep, primitive level.

He was a cowboy, all right. A man's man. A make-your-hormones-jump-up-and-say-yee-hah! kind of man.

Just like the ones in all of the stories Holly's mother had told her when she'd been a little girl.

Minus the hormone-jumping, of course. Holly was the one who'd added the last part after she'd watched Brad Pitt saddle a horse in *Legends of the Fall*. That's when she'd started to cultivate a few stories of her own that were much more naughty than her mother's G-rated versions about the rancher who defended his land against poachers or the sheriff out to save the town's bank from robbers.

Holly's fantasy cowboys were more sexy than noble. Wild as opposed to tame. Wicked instead of virtuous. Hot and unsettling rather than warm and comforting.

She couldn't help but wonder if the man across the room would measure up to all of her erotic dreams.

As if he sensed her attention, he lifted his head. He tilted the brim of his hat back just a hair and his gaze locked with hers. An undercurrent of heat rushed between them. Awareness rippled along her spine and her senses came alive.

The scent of smoke and leather and beer teased her nostrils. The slow, seductive twang of a Kenny Chesney song filtered from the overhead speakers and slid into her ears. The sweet taste of Dr. Pepper lingered in her mouth and she flicked her tongue along the plump fullness of her bottom lip. Her breaths came quicker and she became acutely aware of the tight lace of her bra against her suddenly ripe nipples.

He grinned, just a slow, lazy tilt to his lips, but it was enough to make her mouth go dry. A burst of heat washed from her head to her toes, and left every inch in between panting for more. Her skin grew itchy and tight.

Forget measuring up. He'd already surpassed her expectations, and with nothing more than a glance. Understandable. He wasn't just a face on a movie screen or a red-hot image spicing up her thoughts. He was flesh and blood, and he wanted her back.

Interest gleamed in his gaze, as vivid as the blue neon Bud Lite sign that hung just to his right. He was intrigued, all right. And turned on. And he definitely seemed as if he wanted her.

As much as she wanted him.

She took a long drink of her Dr. Pepper and tried to get a grip on the fierce lust raging inside of her. An emotion the likes of which she'd never felt before.

Then again, it only seemed fitting that what she felt right now would be different from anything in her past.

She'd expected different.

She'd anticipated it.

Because today was a new beginning for Holly Farraday.

It was her first official day in Romeo, Texas.

Up until last week, she'd been running her home-based gourmet dessert business, Sweet & Sinful, out of a sizable apartment in Houston's Galleria area. She'd been right in the middle of lamenting her lack of oven space—she desperately needed a third commercial oven to accommodate her growing customer base—when she'd received the phone call informing her that her grandmother had passed away.

Her *grandmother*. As in a flesh and blood relative. A family that went beyond her own mother who'd died in a car accident when Holly had been eight years old.

Holly's heart paused and disbelief rushed through her yet again. Her mother, while loving and caring, had been very closemouthed when it came to family. Jeanine Farraday had been a runaway, determined to break away from her own mother and her small-town past. She'd never spoken of either, despite her daughter's endless questions.

And so Holly had always wondered. Why had her mother run away? Why had she kept running?

Holly had longed for answers. Even more, she'd yearned for even the smallest connection to anyone beyond her mother. Now she had one. Her ancestors had lived right here in Romeo for the past three generations after immigrating from Ireland.

A tradition that Holly intended to continue thanks to Red Rose Farraday who'd left her a small spread on the outskirts of town.

Excitement rushed through her and her heart pounded faster. A real *home*. A first for Holly who'd been on the run with her mother for the first eight years of her life, and in and out of the foster care system thereafter until she'd turned eighteen. She'd been on her own ever since. She'd worked her way through college and struggled to make something of herself.

It had taken her eight years and a lot of hard work, but she'd finally graduated from the University of Houston with a business degree. She'd spent the next two years working as a pastry chef and trying to save enough money to start her own business. She'd come up short, but with the help of a grant—she'd applied for so many loans and grants that she still couldn't remember the source—she'd been able to buy her equipment and bank six months of living expenses. She'd quit her job and launched Sweet & Sinful. She'd started with five basic aphrodisiac desserts—Ultimate Milk Chocolate Orgasm, Warm Fudge Foreplay, Strawberry Sinsation, Cherry Body Bon Bons and Ooey Gooey Ecstasy—a simple, but tasteful Web site, and a desperate prayer for success. One that had been answered. In three years, she'd managed to add to her dessert list, expand her Web site and actually net a very substantial profit.

While Holly had made something of herself and come a long way from the days when she'd been cold and hungry and penniless, one thing hadn't changed. The isolation she'd felt since her mother—her last living relative, or so she'd thought—had died. The loneliness. The strange feeling that something was still missing from her life.

Until now.

She'd spent the past five years building her business and now it was time to build herself a real home. She wanted to settle down, plant her roots and make some real friends for once in her life.

And so she hadn't even considered the offer made by a nearby neighbor to purchase her grandmother's place.

Instead, she'd signed all of the appropriate papers just that afternoon and was now the official owner of the Farraday Inn, an ancient farmhouse that stood just outside of town on fifty acres of rich, green pastureland.

She'd learned from the lawyer that the house had sat empty for the past ten years—since her grandmother had checked herself into a nursing home because of the heart condition that had eventually claimed her life. But no amount of dust or cobwebs could dissuade Holly from taking up residence. She might be a big-city girl with an addiction to shopping, but she could forego easy access to Neiman Marcus and Saks in the name of home and hearth. She'd watched *The Simple Life*. Country living had its own charm and so she'd mapped out a viable plan for relocating her business and her life.

She intended to use the second story as her personal living quarters. She would operate her business from the first level, using the downstairs bedrooms for storage, packaging and shipping rooms. The cooking itself would be done in the monstrous kitchen that would be more than big enough to accommodate the extra commercial oven Holly intended to purchase just as soon as she set up shop.

A real *home*.

Definitely cause for celebration.

She'd meant to have herself a big piece of chocolate cake or maybe an extremely fattening hot-fudge sundae to celebrate. But the local diner had already closed and the only thing open in Romeo on a Friday night was The Buckin' Bronco Dance Hall, a crowded honky-tonk just this side of the railroad tracks, and the Dusty Saddle Saloon—a tin barn with a hay-strewn floor, a dozen mis-matched tables and chairs, a big-screen television, a pool table, a juke box and an ancient-looking bar. She'd opted for the smaller, more intimate setting of the sa-loon and a soda.

She hadn't counted on the cowboy or the need that blindsided her and turned her upside down and inside out.

She wanted him.

Twenty-four hours ago she would have acted on the feeling. Before Holly had washed her hands of tempo-rary relationships. She'd had too many people come and go in her lifetime and she wasn't about to add one more to the list.

But man-o-man… He *was* hot.

"Now there's a hottie if I ever saw one," a voice ech-oed as if reading Holly's thoughts.

Holly's hand stalled an inch shy of her Dr. Pepper as a six-foot-plus woman with mousy brown hair pulled back in a much too-tight ponytail bumped shoulders with her before settling on the next stool.

The woman wore a red T-shirt and blue jean overalls. Her face was devoid of makeup except for the faint smudge of mascara beneath her eyes, as if she'd cried off the little bit she'd worn. She shimmied on the bar stool and tried to find a comfortable position. Not an easy mission for some-one who'd obviously had a little too much to drink.

"Second-best-looking man in Romeo," the woman went on, her voice slightly slurred. She took a swig from a half-empty bottle of Lonestar beer before mo-tioning across the room to the hot, hunky cowboy near the pool table.

The player controlling the table aimed for a difficult shot. Balls clicked and the eight ball hit the corner pocket with a loud *thunk*. A round of cheers went up. The cowboy grinned, took the pile of cash sitting on the edge of the table and stuffed it into his pocket. He clapped the winning player on the back and exchanged a few words before turning to the loser and shaking the man's hand, as well.

"Second-best?" Holly took another sip of Dr. Pepper and prayed for the ice-cold liquid to cool her hot body. "Who's the first?"

"That would be the most wonderful man in the world. My husband, Bert Wayne." The name ended on a sob. Tears brightened her eyes and spilled over.

"Are you okay?" Holly set her soda on the bar and touched the woman's arm.

"I'm f-fine." The woman tried for a smile that failed miserably. "Better than fine. I'm free—or I will be once Bert Wayne goes through with the divorce proceedings. That's why I'm out living it up on a Saturday night." She motioned around her. "Bert Wayne ain't the only one who knows how to have himself a good time. It's my turn."

"You're entitled."

"That's right. I deserve some fun. I *am* fun." She sniffled again. "Even if Bert Wayne doesn't think so." She caught another sob before shaking her head. "I still can't believe it." Her watery gaze met Holly's. "He said I was boring. That's why he left me for Trana Lee Jenkins—she's the new French manicure technician down at Miss Kim's Nail Salon. He said I just didn't excite him anymore and that he had to move on to greener pastures because mine had dried up and withered away." More tears spilled over and she slapped at them with the back of one hand. "I'm so sorry. You probably don't want to hear any of this."

"It's okay."

"But you don't even know me."

"I know what it's like to be alone." She'd spent most of her life alone. Lonely.

Holly shook away the last thought and smiled. It was a new day. A new life. She'd finally come home. "My name is Holly Farraday."

"I'm Sue Jack—did you say Farraday?" At Holly's nod, she added, "As in *Red Rose* Farraday?"

Holly nodded. "She's my grandmother. Well, she was my grandmother before she passed away. She left me her place. First thing tomorrow, I'm packing up my business and moving everything here."

"You're setting up shop out at Rose's place?"

Holly nodded. "I've been operating from Houston, but the city is so crowded and my place is too small to accommodate all of my customers." When the woman's eyes widened, Holly realized what she must be thinking. After all, Red Rose Farraday hadn't just been Holly's grandmother. She'd also been one of the most notorious madams in Texas history who'd plied her trade at none other than the Farraday Inn.

Oddly enough, her grandmother's notoriety hadn't come as near a shock as the news that she'd had a grandmother in the first place.

"I make desserts for a living," Holly explained. "I sell

through a mail-order catalog and on the Internet. Satis-faction guaranteed or your money back."

Sue teared up again. "I always thought I knew how to satisfy Bert Wayne, but then he up and left. Didn't even say goodbye."

"That's terrible."

"Not really." She sniffled. "I mean, it is terrible, but I don't blame him. He's right. I am dried up. I've been sitting here for three hours and not one man has tried to pick me up. I'm a total loser. I'm a jawbreaker in a candy store full of mouthwatering chocolate. No one in their right mind picks a jawbreaker when they've got wall-to-wall Hershey's Kisses."

"You're not a jawbreaker."

"Yes, I am. I'm a big, fat, round blue jawbreaker." She hiccupped. "On top of that, I'm drunk and I can't drive home."

"You don't have to," Holly said as she climbed from her bar stool. "Let's go."

Sue shook her head. "Thanks, but you shouldn't have to leave and ruin your Saturday night just 'cause of me. I'll just walk. It's not far. Just a few miles up the—whoa," she said as she tried to slide off the bar stool. She teetered and would have fallen flat on her face if Holly hadn't caught her by the arm.

"I think walking is out of the question."

"That's funny," Sue said as she leaned against Holly. "My legs were working just a few minutes ago. It's probably arthritis." She sniffled and sobbed. "That happens when you get old and dried up."

"It's not old age. It's the tequila," a deep voice said.

Holly glanced up just in time to see Mr. Hot and Hunky Cowboy walk up next to her. He gave Holly a smile and a wink that stalled her heart before turning to Sue.

"Hey there, Josh," Sue said, a smile warming her face as she glanced up.

"Hey there, Sue. You look mighty nice tonight."

"You're just saying that." But she smiled anyway. "Josh McGraw, have you met Heidi. Or is it Hominy? Or Hailey?"

"My name is Holly," she told Josh.

"Nice to meet you, Holly." The name rolled off his tongue, so deep and husky, and heat rushed through her body. Her nipples pebbled and pressed against the lace of her bra. "You need a lift home, Sue?"

"Hannah's takin' me." Sue beamed at Holly. "She's my new friend."

"That's right," Holly said. "Let me just pay for my soda and—oomph!" she groaned as Sue teetered, threatening to pull them both to the ground if the cowboy hadn't reached out and steadied the woman again.

"I'll help you get her to the car," Josh told Holly. He motioned to the bartender. "Put everything on my tab."

Sue's eyes teared up again as Josh slid an arm around her and hefted her to her feet. "You're so nice," she told the cowboy. "Bert Wayne was nice, too. But then he got bored and I got fat and…" She rambled on as Josh steered her after Holly who headed for the exit.

A few minutes later, Josh settled Sue into the passenger seat of Holly's champagne-colored Lincoln Navigator. He clicked her seat belt into place, closed the door and rounded the front.

"Nice wheels," he said, trailing his hand over the hood as he rounded the front of her SUV.

"Thanks. I got it in Houston."

"Is that where you're from?"

She nodded. "Thanks for the help," she told him as he came around to the driver's side where she stood. "I don't know how I would have done it without you."

"No problem." He stopped just inches shy of her. So close she could feel the heat coming off his body and smell the faint scent of beer and leather that clung to him. "Sue's not usually like this," he went on. "She's just having a hard time. She's been pretty torn up since Bert Wayne moved out and filed for divorce."

"I know the feeling."

He arched an eyebrow at her. "You know what it's like to have a cheating husband?"

"I know what it's like to be alone. I've been that way most of my life." Until now.

She had a home now. And she intended to plant roots and make friends.

Starting now.

"So you *don't* have a husband, cheating or otherwise?" he asked her.

"No."

"Boyfriend?"

"Not at the present time."

"Girlfriend?"

She grinned. "No. How about you?"

"No girlfriend or boyfriend."

"A wife?"

"I don't have one of those, either."

"That's good." The lust she'd felt inside the bar returned in full force and she forgot all about her vow to hold back and take things slow and… *Permanent.* Her nipples throbbed and heat flooded between her legs and she had the sudden urge to lean up on her tiptoes and touch her lips to his to see if he tasted half as delicious as he looked.

She leaned up and he leaned down and—

"The car is spinning," Sue said from inside.

Holly froze, her mouth just inches shy of touching his, and licked her lips. "I, um, think I'd better be going."

"Let's go."

"I thought I was driving her home."

"Do you know where she lives?" When she shook her head, he ducked his head to glance in at Sue who'd tilted her head back on the seat and closed her eyes. She murmured something incoherent and whimpered. "I don't think she's going to be much help. I'll drive."

Holly handed him her keys and climbed into the backseat. She settled into the soft leather as Josh McGraw climbed behind the wheel of her Lincoln Navigator, started the engine and pulled out of the gravel parking lot.

The drive took less than five minutes, but it was the longest of Holly's life. He was too close, too tempting, his gaze too disturbing every time he glanced in the rearview mirror and eyed her.

Awareness rippled along her spine and heat fluttered over her nerve endings. Her stomach hollowed out and a hunger, fierce and demanding, settled inside. It was one thing to watch him from afar, and quite another to have him just an arm's reach away.

So close all she had to do was reach out and…

She wouldn't. Not really. But in her mind's eye, she leaned over the edge of the seat and touched the soft strands of dark hair that brushed his collar. Her fingers dipped beneath and grazed the hot flesh of his neck. Her palm trailed over the leather strap of his choker, tracing it toward the front. She undid the first button of his shirt. The hard muscle of his chest met her palm as she leaned over him and moved lower, down his rippled abdomen, around the indentation of his belly button to the waistband of his jeans. With a flick of her wrist, she eased the button open and urged his zipper over his erection. She tugged at the elastic of his briefs and slid her fingers beneath and—

"We're here." His deep voice drew her from her thoughts. Her head snapped up and her gaze collided with his. A fierce light gleamed in his blue gaze, as if he knew where her thoughts had almost taken her. As if he were already there, waiting and burning and wanting.

She cleared her throat and slid from the backseat as Josh climbed out of the car and went to help Sue from the passenger's side.

It took fifteen minutes to get Sue settled inside her house before they finally climbed back into the Navigator, Josh back in the driver's seat. He keyed the ignition, gunned the engine and pulled out of the gravel driveway. A few seconds later, they reached the stop sign at the end of Sue's street.

"What are you doing?" she asked him when he just sat there, engine idling, as if he didn't know which way to turn.

He stared straight ahead at the quiet expanse of road. "Wondering."

"Wondering what?"

"If I should head back to the bar, or if I should head for the interstate and the nearest motel."

The bar, her conscience whispered. The last thing she needed was to start the permanent phase of her life with a one-night stand.

Then again, a one-night stand was someone that you slept with and never saw again. This guy was obviously local. In a town this small, she would be seeing him again. And again.

A problem in and of itself.

Her head knew that and it started to send a warning south to all of the relevant body parts.

But then his gaze caught hers and there was no mistaking the heat that burned in the dark depths. Her breath caught and her body throbbed and the words were out before she could stop them. "I *could* use a good mini-bar right about now."

2

JOSH MCGRAW'S hands actually trembled as he shoved the key into the lock after registering them at the Lone Ranger Motel, a clean but ancient establishment just outside the city limits. It had been a long, long time since he'd been this worked up. This hot. This hard. This...*desperate*.

The knowledge would have been enough to send him running for the next county if the circumstances had been different—if Holly had been any of the dozen or so "Juliets," Romeo's official organization of single women—who'd been in hot pursuit since he'd returned to town six months ago for his grandfather's funeral.

Hell, they'd been after him even before then. Since he'd turned thirteen and played his first game of hide-and-seek with Dana Louise Shipley. Not the traditional version, mind you. The game he'd played with Dana had involved hiding a certain body *part,* and had caused quite a stir when the captain of the cheerleader squad had found them out behind the bleachers during a pep rally and let loose a scream. He'd been just one of the rough and tumble McGraw triplets—an unruly trio notorious for making noise and breaking rules—until damn near every female at Romeo High had gotten a glimpse of him naked. He'd gone from a troublemaker to a lovemaker in the blink of an eye, and he'd had a ready supply of females ever since.

The trouble was, where they'd once wanted a good time back in high school, they now wanted a walk down the aisle. Marriage. Forever.

Hell, no.

Josh wasn't the marrying type any more than all of the McGraw men who'd come before him. From his great-grandfather who'd had not one, but two mistresses, to his grandfather who'd kept company with Red Rose Farraday herself—the notorious madam and owner of Romeo's very own house of ill repute—to his own father who'd had affair after affair.

Unlike them, however, Josh wasn't going to ignore his shortcomings and make false promises by saying "I do." Instead, he made it a point to stay single, which meant steering clear of the Juliets who wanted commitment in addition to sex.

So for the past six months, he'd traveled the few hours to Austin whenever the urge overwhelmed him and visited any one of the handful of women he'd developed a physical relationship with over the past years. The knowledgeable sort who took their own pleasure and didn't rely on him to tease and tantalize and coax them into an orgasm.

Making the trip every so often wasn't exactly convenient, but it was a damned sight more safe than getting lassoed by a disillusioned Juliet who thought he was the answer to all of her romantic prayers.

He wasn't. He was just a man. Selfish on occasion. Egotistical most of the time. Hardheaded all of the time. And too friggin' lusty—thanks to the McGraw bloodline—to commit himself to one female for the rest of his born days.

Josh liked his freedom and he liked playing the field.

Even more, he wasn't of a mind to hurt anyone.

He'd done that once before and he'd lived with the guilt ever since.

His gaze slid to the woman who stood beside him. She wasn't tall, but she wasn't small, either, with a pair of two-inch black stiletto heels that made her legs seem endless before they reached the short black skirt that molded to her round ass. A white silk tank hugged her luscious breasts. Her soft red hair hung down around her shoulders and framed her heart-shaped face. Her lips were full and pink, her green eyes hot and bright, and his cock twitched in anticipation.

Holly with her high heels and expensive clothes and fancy SUV wasn't one of the women in town. She was a stranger. She was single. And judging by the way she licked her lips, she wanted the same thing from him that he wanted from her—sex.

He pushed open the door, stepped back and let her precede him inside. He expected more of an exotic fragrance from her given her big-city appearance. Instead, the warm scent of sugar and vanilla filled his nostrils as she eased past him. She smelled like sweet, fresh-from-the-oven cupcakes and his nostrils flared. A warning sounded somewhere in the back of his brain, but it wasn't loud enough to push past the sudden hammering of his heart. A bolt of need shot through his body and his muscles bunched. He barely resisted the urge to haul her into his arms, back her up against the wall and take her hard and fast right there under the bare porch light, the june bugs bumping overhead.

As appealing as the notion, the thought of laying her down on a soft mattress and peeling away her clothes one piece at a time suddenly made him even hotter. Harder.

He followed her inside, closing the door behind them. A *click* sounded as she turned on a nearby lamp. A pale yellow glow pushed back the shadows and illuminated the interior. The room was far from fancy, but it was neat and clean. An unfinished pine dresser sat in the far corner, an ancient-looking television rested on top. A king-size bed took up the rest of the space. Beige curtains patterned with silver spurs covered the one window near a window air-conditioning unit. A matching comforter covered the bed. The slightly scarred hardwood floor gleamed from a recent polishing.

"I don't see a minibar," he said as his gaze swept the interior. "But if you're hungry there's a vending machine around the corner near the ice machine. I could get you something."

She eyed him. "It was just a figure of speech. I wasn't really in the mood to raid the minibar."

"Then what are you in the mood for?"

"I…" She licked her lips and he had the gut feeling that she'd never done this sort of thing before. And then his gaze caught hers and he knew deep down that this was, indeed, a first for her.

His blood rushed even faster at the notion. A crazy

reaction because Josh wasn't in the habit of being the first anything when it came to women. Be it a first lover or a first one-night stand or the first man to actually cause an orgasm. Rather, he steered clear of any situation that might set him apart in a woman's mind and make him more than just a really good lay.

He stiffened, his fingers tightening on the room key. "Maybe this isn't such a good idea."

"You're right about that." The hesitant light in her gaze faded into a wave of bright green heat as she stepped closer. "It's not good at all." Another step and her nipples kissed his chest.

The one touch shifted him into high speed. He pulled her close and thrust his tongue into the heated depths of her mouth, kissing her, devouring her.

His hands massaged her soft, round ass and he rubbed his throbbing erection against the cradle of her pelvis. His fingers bunched material until he reached the hem of the skirt and felt her bare flesh beneath. Her thighs were hot to the touch. Soft. Quivering.

Holy hell.

Urging her backward, he eased her down onto the bed. He captured her mouth in a deep, intense kiss that lasted several heartbeats before he pulled away and stepped back. He worked the buttons free on his shirt and let the material slide from his shoulders. He unfastened the button on his jeans and pushed the zipper down. The pressure eased and the edges gaped and he could actually breathe for a few seconds.

Until she pushed to a sitting position and leaned forward.

Her fingers touched the dark purple head of his erection where it pushed up above the waistband of his briefs. The air lodged in his throat and he ground his teeth against a burst of white-hot pleasure. Her touch was so damned soft and he was so hard and…

He needed to touch her. To see her.

He reached for the hem of her tank top and pulled it up and over her head. One dark red nipple pushed through the lace-patterned cup of her white bra. He leaned over and flicked his tongue over the rock-hard tip. She gasped and he drew the nub deeper into his mouth, sucking her hard through the flimsy covering.

Her fingers threaded through his hair and held him close. He relished the taste of her flesh for several heart-pounding moments before he pulled away. He gripped the cups of her bra and pulled them down and under the fullness of her breasts. The bra plumped her and her ripe nipples raised in invitation. When he didn't lower his head and suckle her again, she reached for him.

"Please."

"Easy, darlin'. We'll get to it." But not yet. He wasn't a man to take his good fortune for granted. It was a rare occasion when a man found a woman like her at a hole-in-the-wall in such a desperately small town.

He meant to take his time and enjoy the looking and the touching and the anticipation.

He unzipped her skirt and peeled it from her body in a slow, tantalizing motion that stirred goose bumps on her soft flesh. Trailing his fingers back up the way they'd come, he hooked his fingers at the thin straps of her panties and followed the same path down her long legs.

When he had her naked with the exception of the bra pulled beneath her luscious breasts, he leaned up and let his gaze sweep the length of her.

She was definitely not from around here, he realized when his attention settled on the barely there strip of pubic hair that told him she'd been pampered and waxed at some fine salon rather than Miss Millie's Hair Barn. As advertised on the marquee outside of her shop, Miss Millie's waxing services didn't extend any farther south than unruly chin hairs for which she ran a weekly special.

"Did you get this in Houston, too?" He trailed a finger down the barely there strip of hair and watched her tremble.

"Yes."

"It's nice." He traced the slit that separated her lush pink lips and she caught her bottom lip as a groan trembled from her mouth. Her legs fell open and the soft pink flesh parted for him.

He dipped his fingertip into her steamy heat and watched her pupils dilate. Her mouth opened and she gasped. And then he went deeper, until her eyes fluttered closed again and her head fell back. He worked her, sliding his finger in and out until her essence coated his flesh and a drop trickled down his palm.

Hunger raged inside him and he dipped his head, flicked his tongue over the swollen tissue and lapped up her sweet juice.

At the first contact of his mouth, she arched up off the bed and her hands grasped his head. He tasted her, savoring the bitter sweetness and relishing the sound of a gasp here and a moan there. He swirled his tongue around her clitoris and felt the tip ripen for him. She whimpered as he sucked the sensitive nub into his mouth and nibbled until she tensed beneath him. Her fingers clutched at his hair in a grip that was just short of painful. The sensation fed his ravenous desire and made his breath quicken. He laved her once, twice and her breath caught on a ragged gasp. He knew she was close.

So close, but not quite there.

He gathered his control and pulled away, determined to make it last for the both of them. But then his gaze collided with hers and he saw the fierce glitter in her eyes—a mix of desire and relief and a desperate longing—and he had the strange feeling that this moment meant more than just sating her lust.

As if she weren't just living in the moment, but looking forward to the morning after.

If he had been a different man, he might have liked the notion. But Josh McGraw wasn't interested in a future when it came to women. The only thing on his mind was fulfilling his grandfather's dying wish, and getting the hell out of Romeo and back to his life.

His gaze shifted to her naked body. Okay, so it wasn't the *only* thing on his mind at the moment, but it was still a priority.

Right beneath getting inside the hot, sexy woman stretched out on the bed.

He snatched up his jeans and retrieved a condom from his pocket. After sliding on the latex, he settled between her legs. Bracing himself, he shoved his penis deep into her wet heat in one swift thrust that stalled the air in his lungs.

He gripped her lush hips, his tanned fingers digging into her pale flesh as he plunged into her again. She closed her eyes, lifted her hips and met each thrust until he couldn't take it anymore. His cock throbbed and filled and he was right there. Just a few more movements and he was going to explode….

And she wasn't.

She wasn't nearly as tense, her body wasn't strung as tight as it should have been if she were teetering on the edge.

All the better. If she didn't have an explosive orgasm, it would surely sour the evening and push him right back down to the nothing-special category when it came to men.

He thrust again and again. The pressure built and pleasure fogged his brain and before he could stop himself, he reached down between them and parted her flesh just above the point where he filled her. He caught her swollen clitoris between his thumb and forefinger and squeezed lightly.

She moaned and her body convulsed around him and he knew she'd tumbled over the edge. He buried himself deep one last time and followed. He held her tight and relished the way her inner muscles milked him.

Finally, his hold loosened and he collapsed onto his back. He reached for her, tucking her against his body.

He needed to get up and get dressed. He had an early day waiting for him. He was riding fence first thing in the morning before he moved two hundred new head of cattle into the west pasture. But damned if he could breathe, much less move, and so he closed his eyes. Just for a few minutes. Then he would haul himself up, pull on his clothes and say goodbye.

AN HOUR LATER Josh forced his eyes open just in time to see Holly stand and slide on her panties. He folded his arms behind his head and watched as she bent over to search through the covers they'd kicked off for the rest of her clothes.

She was just pulling on her top when she noticed that he was watching her.

She smiled. "I didn't mean to wake you."

He winked. "I didn't mean to fall asleep."

"It's just that I really need to get going. I've got a long drive ahead of me."

"You're going all the way back to Houston tonight?"

She nodded and finished with the last button before perching on the edge of the bed to pull on her skirt. "I run my own business and I've got a ton of things to do first thing in the morning." She stood and reached for her purse. "Maybe we could have dinner some time. Whenever you're available. I know you're probably busy with horses or cattle or whatever you do."

"Actually, I do both. For now. My grandfather passed away about six months ago and I've been running my family's ranch since then. But that's just temporary until my brother comes home in a few weeks. Then I'm headed back to Arizona. I run a small charter business."

"I thought you were a cowboy."

"Professionally, I'm a pilot."

"But you look like a cowboy."

"Cowboying isn't something you do, cupcake. It's the way you think." He winked. "I'll always be a cowboy. I just like climbing into the cockpit of a Cessna more than I like climbing into a saddle."

Disappointment filled her gaze and Josh barely ignored the urge to pull her into his arms.

"But you look like a cowboy," she stated again, as if she had to say it twice for the words to really sink in. "I'm sorry. I thought…" She shook her head. "Maybe I'll see you around sometime then."

"I doubt that. I don't get down to Houston too often. Austin's closer, so I do most of the ranch business there."

"I'm talking about here. In town. I live here now."

He sat up. "What did you say?"

"As of three o'clock this afternoon, I own the Farraday Inn—my grandmother left it to me."

What? "You're Holly *Farraday?*" It was more of a statement than a question, because the truth was right there in front of him. In the deep red hue of her hair. The bright green of her eyes. He'd recognized her, all right, because she looked like her grandmother. A young, vibrant version of the old woman who'd stolen his grandfather's heart all those years ago, and his land.

"So maybe we'll see each other again," she said as she hauled open the door. "Before you leave, that is."

But there was no maybe about it.

Josh would have to see her again, all right, because sweet-smelling Holly Farraday had something he wanted really, *really* bad.

His groin throbbed and he conceded. Okay, so she had two things he wanted, but he'd already had one of them and he wasn't going back for seconds.

More importantly, she had his family's land and he meant to get it back. He'd promised his grandfather as much, and Josh always kept his word.

Especially with his own peace of mind hanging in the balance.

3

"IT'S ABOUT TIME you showed up." Holly dusted the flour from her blouse as she pulled open the front door of the massive farmhouse. "I'm on my tenth Ultimate Orgasm and I need at least a dozen more."

"I could guarantee one." The voice, deep and husky, slid into her ears as she came face-to-face with the cowboy standing on her doorstep. "Maybe even two or three," he went on, "if I'm not too worked up and there's no vanilla icing involved. But a dozen is pushing it. Even for a McGraw."

"I was talking about an Ultimate Milk Chocolate Orgasm."

"I didn't know they came in flavors."

"Mine do. Milk chocolate." She tried to gather her wits. "I thought you were the UPS guy."

"Cupcake," he said as he leaned one palm against the door frame and stared down at her, "do I look like the UPS guy?"

"No. Yes." She shook her head. "If we were back in Houston, I would say no. But we're here in Timbuktu, where my mailman rides a four-wheeler with a horn that plays 'The Yellow Rose of Texas.' So a UPS guy who looks like the Marlboro Man and drives a…" she glanced past him to the black Dodge Dualie pickup that sat in the front drive "…monster truck wouldn't surprise me in the least."

He grinned and her heart stalled for a dangerous second. Heat skittered along her nerve endings and she had half a mind to reach out and trace the shape of his lips. The other half of her mind voted to bypass the tracing entirely and go straight to a kiss. A hot, wet, deep kiss that would satisfy the sudden craving deep in her belly.

A full-fledged *craving* that had haunted her the entire weekend, when she hadn't had more than a hankering in the past few years since she'd started Sweet & Sinful. Launching a new business left little time for socializing and so she'd been having a major dry spell when it came to sex.

Until Josh McGraw.

He'd quenched her thirst on Friday night, or so she'd thought until she'd spent the past two days wanting another drink.

She'd tried her usual remedy for a bad case of lust— a few spoonfuls of her Ultimate Milk Chocolate Orgasm batter never failed to kill the urge and keep her on the straight and narrow to the land of the financially secure. That and a few private fantasies featuring one of her favorite actors.

Neither had satisfied her this time.

Josh eyed her and awareness skittered along her nerve endings. "Do you usually proposition the UPS guy?"

"Proposition?" Her mind rushed back and she remembered her words. "Oh, you mean the Ultimate Orgasm."

"A dozen of them." He shook his head and grinned. "If your UPS guy can deliver that, he's definitely in the wrong line of work."

"I can see your point." She couldn't help but smile. "But I wasn't referring to that kind of orgasm. The Ultimate Orgasm is a mousse cake," she told him. "Made with three different textures of chocolate, fudge and a sweet cream. It's my top seller—particularly the milk chocolate flavor. I make specialty desserts for a living."

He arched an eyebrow at her. "And here I thought you might be continuing the family tradition."

"I might not agree with my grandmother's choice of profession, but it was her choice." A choice that had obviously forced her only child to run away.

Holly now realized why her mother had been so tight-lipped all those years ago. She'd moved them from city to city, state to state, because she'd been desperate to escape her past and protect her own child from such an influence. Maybe she'd feared her own mother finding her and forcing her back. Or maybe she'd simply been embarrassed. Maybe both. Either way, she'd run and she'd kept running, and now Holly understood.

Not that Holly felt any shame. Sex wasn't held in the same taboo as it had been years ago. Besides, Holly had grown up in the city. Several to be exact. She was more open-minded. But growing up the daughter of a small-town madam... That must have been hard.

"It was her choice," she said again, "and obviously a pretty smart choice, from what I hear." And she'd heard an earful in the few days she'd been in town. There wasn't a person in town who didn't have something to say about the Farraday Inn. Holly had expected negative comments. Instead, she'd been bombarded with questions about Rose and her infamous recipe book—the sexual dishes she'd served up at the Farraday Inn.

Did it exist?

What were the recipes?

Could they really drive a man to the brink of insanity?

Maybe. Holly didn't know. She'd barely set up her kitchen, much less picked her way through her grandmother's belongings. She did know that there were five "dining" rooms upstairs, each decorated with a particular theme that no doubt catered to a particular recipe. As for the recipes themselves... She'd been too busy setting up shop and thinking about Josh McGraw to wonder if such a book still existed.

"My grandmother was very successful at what she did, but I'm not continuing the family tradition. I do my best work in the kitchen."

He reached out, his finger scooping a speck of fudge from her chin. He touched it to his lips. "I'll have to remember that." His gaze went past her to the boxes that filled the living room. "So you're really settling in here?"

"I needed more space for my business. My apartment in Houston barely had room to accommodate a commercial oven. Here I've got room for three."

"Which is why you turned down my offer to buy the place."

She remembered the lawyer's mention of a prospective buyer. "That was you?"

He shrugged. "The floor you're standing on used to belong to the McGraws until your grandmother sweet-talked my grandpa into giving her a piece." His gaze locked with hers. "A piece in return for a piece."

She fought down a wave of anger and smiled instead. "It's a shame your grandfather was such a weak man."

He stared at her as if he wanted to argue, but then his expression softened. "He had his moments. We all do." Regret flashed in his gaze and she might have thought he referred to Friday night, but something in her gut told her the emotion went way beyond one night of lust.

"I'm sorry your grandfather couldn't keep his head, but that has nothing to do with me."

"I'm more than willing to pay what it's worth. The going rate for this area is twenty-thousand an acre. That's what I offered Humphries. But I'm willing to go twenty-five. Plus a nice chunk for this house. I can have the papers drawn up and the money in your hand by the close of business today."

"But I just moved in."

His gaze pushed past her and settled on the stack of boxes sitting in the living room. "You haven't even unpacked."

"I'm unpacking as soon as I get this order out. Not that it matters. I moved here because I want to live here. This is my place now and it's not for sale."

He frowned. "Not for twenty-five thousand an acre. That's what you're saying, right? You want more."

"This place isn't for sale."

"Cupcake, everything's for sale if the price is right. If I've learned anything over the past five years since I started buying back the land that your grandmother gave away, it's that. I actually paid for a five-acre tract on the other side of the river with a custom-made pool and big-screen projection TV. Old Mrs. Witherspoon, whose husband was one of your grandma Rose's favorite customers, said she didn't feel right taking money for something that she didn't rightly pay for—Rose gave it to her husband in appreciation for forty years of loyal patronage."

"If she's got that much of a conscience, I would think she would have just given it back to you."

"She's a good woman, not a stupid one. Besides, she loves *Wheel of Fortune* and her eyesight is fading. That's why she's living in town with her daughter's family. She has trouble getting around by herself and so she spends most of her time sitting around. She needed a big screen she could actually see and she sure-as-shootin' can't afford one on Social Security."

"What about the swimming pool?"

"She's got grandkids and it gets awful hot here in the high heat of summer." For emphasis, he pulled off his hat and wiped a hand over his brow. "It's only May right now and we're already up into the nineties. And this is nothing compared to how hot it's going to get in the next few months."

"I've lived in Houston for five years. I know how hot it gets in Texas. That's why I've ordered two extra window units for the downstairs alone. As for a big screen, I don't have time to watch TV." She had not only her business to keep her busy, but her new life, as well. She needed to really settle in and turn the Farraday Inn into a real home. "I've got curtains to buy and a garden to plant."

"You garden?"

"Not yet, actually, but I'm going to start."

"There are a lot of nice places closer to town."

"I'm sure there are, but I'm not interested."

"Because I haven't hit on the right price. Just tell me what it would take."

She thought for a moment and a smile tugged at her lips. "If you've got one hundred pounds of flour on you, I might be willing to make a deal."

"A *hundred* pounds?"

"I've got orders to fill and I'm crunched for time." She glanced at her watch. "I really have to go. So unless you're packing several bags of the white stuff, this conversation is over."

She could tell that he wanted to smile. But something held him back. "That's your final answer?"

"Yes." She watched him shrug as if giving in. *Yeah, right.* If she'd learned anything over the past two days, it was that Josh McGraw was a man who went after what he wanted. She'd heard almost as many rumors about him as she had her grandmother. About how he and his two brothers—he was the oldest of triplets—had practically ruled the town back in the day before they'd all gone off their separate ways. She'd heard about his parents' untimely deaths within twenty-four hours of each other and his grandfather's diagnosis with prostate cancer five years ago and the old man's death just six months ago. All three boys had come back for their grandfather's funeral, but Josh had been the only one to come sooner. He'd spent time with his grandfather during his last days, and he'd stayed on to run the ranch and buy back the fragmented pieces.

Yes, she'd heard about him, all right.

After she'd asked.

"I realize you're set on living here, but it's not going to be the same as the city," he went on. His gaze fell to the pink strappy sandals she'd pulled on that morning, along with a pink miniskirt and a white T-shirt that read Princess in pink glitter. A perfect ensemble for the mall. Not so perfect for a house out in the middle of nowhere. "You might not like it."

"If you're trying to discourage me, it won't work."

"Why's that?"

"Because I've already given myself the same speech. I know why I shouldn't be here. The thing is, I *want* to be here." Which was why she'd bought herself a pair of cowboy boots with a tastefully low heel and several pairs of jeans. She just hadn't been able to find them amid all of the other boxes cluttering up the house.

He stared her up and down, a sweeping gaze that seemed to pause at all of her hot spots, before he finally shrugged. "You can't blame a guy for trying."

"Why do I have a feeling this isn't your final offer?" she asked him.

He smiled and tipped his hat. "Because it's not, cupcake. I'll definitely be seeing you around."

"Not if I see you first," she breathed as she closed the

door behind her and leaned back for a long, heart-pounding moment.

Josh McGraw was not conducive to her peace of mind. He distracted her. Worse, he attracted her. Enough to make her think twice about what he'd said.

You might not like it.

Ridiculous. She would like it. She would love it because this was her dream—a real home where she could plant a garden and make friends and finally fit in for the first time in her life. It was the lust that made her blow out a deep breath and notice the dampness of her T-shirt and the sweat that trickled down her temple.

She'd lived in Texas for several years. She was used to the heat. Of course, it was quite a bit hotter here than it had been in Houston. And her apartment building had been fairly new, with central-air units in each apartment. Unlike the old farmhouse and its one ancient window unit.

That's just temporary. Like Josh.

Holly was through with fast and furious when it came to relationships. She wanted lasting relationships from here on out. From friendships to that special someone.

For the first time in her life, she wanted a special someone. A man to laugh with, grow old with, *love*.

She licked her lips and tried to ignore the tingling of her own bottom lip as she headed back to her kitchen.

JOSH CLIMBED into his truck and headed down the long stretch of driveway toward the small farm road that connected the Farraday Inn with the Iron Horse Ranch, and tried to catch his breath.

She'd turned him down. At the same time, just seeing her had turned him on. And hearing her say the word orgasm… That hadn't helped the situation even if she had been talking about a dessert.

When he pictured a woman who baked for a living, the first image that came to mind was his great-aunt Lurline. She'd made the best peanut butter cookies this side of the Rio Grande. She was also eighty-two with a soft, plump body and a steel-gray perm.

Holly Farraday, on the other hand, had a body made for hot, sweaty bumping and grinding. Long legs that wrapped around his waist and refused to let go. A soft, round ass that fit his hands just perfect. A smooth belly that felt whisper soft against his lips. Perky breasts that plumped in his hands and red nipples that ripened at the flick of his tongue.

His fingers flexed on the steering wheel. Restlessness clawed at his insides as he turned the truck onto the main road and pressed down on the accelerator. The engine roared to life, eating up gravel and dust at a frantic pace that matched his heartbeat.

He'd had a hunch she wouldn't sell the moment she'd suggested dinner on Friday night after they'd had sex. Dinner meant tomorrow and tomorrow meant next week, and next week meant that he was shit out of luck. But he'd promised his grandfather, and himself, and so he'd swallowed his skepticism and driven out to the Farraday Inn today and made his offer.

And then another. And another.

And the whole friggin' time, the only thing he'd been thinking of was, not how much he wanted the land, but how much he wanted her.

Under him, surrounding him, squeezing his cock with her sweet heat until he couldn't think anymore.

Not about the past and his own mistake that still ate away inside of him. Not about the present and fixing his grandfather's mistake. And not about the future and the guilt that would stay with him for the rest of his life if he didn't make amends right now and put the Iron Horse back together.

He might not be able to do it.

Before he had a chance to dwell on the realization, his cell phone rang.

Josh checked the caller ID and pressed the talk button. "How's it hangin', bro?"

"It isn't." Mason McGraw's voice floated over the line. "It's gone into permanent hiding."

"Don't tell me you've got a pissed-off father on your tail."

"Worse."

Josh started to ask about a pissed-off husband, but he knew better. While he and his brothers had varied tastes when it came to women—Josh went for the temporary beauties who steered free of commitment, Mason had a thing for party-hearty, blue-eyed blondes with big breasts, while Rance liked them tall and classy—they all lived by one rule. No married women. "Two pissed-off fathers?" he asked instead.

"I wish. Try a kindergarten teacher with a really loud biological clock."

"Since when do you do schoolteachers?"

"I didn't do her. We're just friends. At least, I thought we were up until last night when she asked me if I liked the name Jason. I said yes and she said good because it's the name she's picked out for baby number one. I haven't even kissed her and she's talking babies, for chrissake. I can't have a kid right now. I mean, someday, sure. But now? And when I do, I'm sure as hell not going to name him Jason. It's an all right name, but my boy is going to be a junior—"

"Whoa, back up a second. You and this teacher are just *friends?* As in order a pizza, watch the game and share a few beers?"

"This is the Black Hills, bro. I'm smack-dab in the middle of a five-thousand-acre ranch centered around a small town, population eight hundred. The closest pizza place is a good three hours away. She offered to cook." When Josh let loose a loud whistle, Mason added, "Look, it's not like that. At least I didn't think it was like that. I see her every now and then when I go into town. She knows I'm from Texas and she likes the Houston Texans. We talk football. At least we did talk football until last night."

"What did she cook?"

"What difference does it make?"

"Well, if she served you a Hungry Man, I'd say you're probably overreacting. TV dinners don't require the same commitment as real food."

"She made stew."

"Uh-oh."

"And home-baked rolls."

"You're totally screwed," Josh told him. "Unless you clean the slate right now. Turn down the next dinner date."

"That's not an option."

"Why not?"

"Because I already said yes. I started to say no, but then she looked like she was going to cry and I buckled. Christ, I need to hurry the hell up and get out of here."

"How much longer?"

"We're inseminating the last batch of cattle next week. After that, it's just paperwork and planning. I should wrap everything up in about three to four weeks. Five at the most. What am I going to do?"

"Get used to the name Jason."

"Kiss my ass."

Josh laughed. "It's good to see the stress hasn't affected your charm." An idea struck just as he said the words. "That's it, bro."

"What are you talking about?"

"You're stuck in this situation because you're not looking at this woman as a woman. I'm assuming she's nowhere near Triple B status."

"She's a brunette. Brown eyes. Good sense of humor. Smart. I'm not sure about her figure because she wears these loose, overall type dresses like Ms. Crenshaw." Ms. Crenshaw had been their third-grade teacher. She'd worn thick, chunky black shoes and said, "Sit up straight!" in a voice that had made even the McGraw brothers snap to attention. "She might have a decent chest. I don't know. I don't think of her like that."

"So start. She obviously thinks you're this nice, professional, mild-mannered sort of guy who likes animals. While you do like animals, you're also capable of acting like one."

"I never really thought about it like that. It'll take

some effort—she actually told me to sit up straight at dinner last night—but I can do it."

"And do it fast."

"You anxious to leave already?"

"I'm anxious for a good night's sleep. I've got Uncle Eustace and Aunt Lurline arguing down the hall every night." And one sweet, sexy-as-hell woman now haunting his thoughts.

"Just keep your pants on and I'll be there soon."

Too late, Josh thought as he punched the end button and slid the phone onto the dashboard. *Too friggin' late.*

A HALF HOUR after closing the door on Josh, Holly eyed the rich fudge dessert she'd just removed from the oven. She'd run out of flour halfway through the recipe and so the cake had turned out more ho-hum than extreme. The edges sagged and the middle had caved in enough to give it a lopsided look. She pinched the edge and popped it into her mouth.

Rich chocolate exploded on her tongue and tantalized her taste buds for a long, heart-pounding moment. Not bad for ho-hum. Then again, she wasn't an adequate judge at the moment, not with her senses still buzzing from a certain tall, dark and delicious cowboy.

His image pushed into her mind and heat swept through her body. Her hands trembled and her insides went all tight and itchy.

She turned toward the mixing bowl where she'd whipped up the concoction a half hour ago. Rich batter still coated the sides and her stomach growled. She grabbed a spoon and scraped one side before taking a bite. Where one was usually enough to kill any frustration eating away inside her, she had to scrape the entire bowl and lick both beaters before she felt even marginally satisfied.

She ate another spoonful for good measure before setting the empty bowl and beaters in the sink. The doorbell rang just as she turned to her computer to track her supply order.

"Finally," she breathed as she hauled open the door to find a handful of women standing on her front porch.

"Welcome to Romeo," they announced in unison.

"I'm Lolly Mae Langtree," said the thirtysomething blonde standing in the middle. "President of the Juliets. We're *the* organization for the single women in town. We coordinate with the Elks and the other men's groups to plan mixers and give our members a chance to get out and meet Mr. Right." She handed Holly a large, white, wrapped box decorated with a big, pink bow. "On behalf of everyone, I'd like to welcome you to Romeo." She gave Holly a fierce hug. "We are *so* excited to have Rose's very own granddaughter with us. It's such a shame how the townsfolk used to treat her—the women, I mean—but you don't have to worry a thing about that. This isn't the Dark Ages anymore and we don't sit around doing needlepoint and blaming Rose for the lack of commitment-minded men in town like the Juliets before us."

"That's right. We're really into quilting now, and we aren't the least bit threatened by your know-how."

"What Marcia Renee is trying to say," Lolly offered, "is that we respect you on a professional level."

"That's right," one of the other women chimed in. "We know you're not here to drain the pool of available men."

"What Cookie Michelle is trying to say," Lolly added, "is that we know you're here in a purely professional capacity."

"I make aphrodisiac desserts," Holly said. "That's my profession."

"Of course, it is," Lolly told her as she moved past her into the living room, a look of awe on her face. "So this is it." She turned. "It doesn't look a thing like I expected."

"There isn't an ounce of crushed red velvet anywhere," another of the women said, her gaze open and excited. "Jennifer Susan Fitch," she told Holly. "Pleased to make your acquaintance." Her attention traveled the room. "I always thought there'd be crushed velvet. There's always crushed velvet in all of the old Mae West movies."

"True, but how can you tell it's red crushed velvet?" another woman asked. "It could be orange or purple or even blue. The films are all in black and white, so there's no way to really know." She perched on the edge of the plastic-wrapped sofa just delivered yesterday.

"Red is risqué," Jennifer said as she followed the woman's lead and seated herself. "It *has* to be red."

"You only say that because you just redecorated your bedroom in red and you're hoping it'll work on Charlie."

"I am not. First off, Charlie and I have only had two dates. He certainly hasn't seen my bedroom at this point. But when he does, he'll be swept away with passion because red is a sensual color. Red says sex. Hot, vibrant,

exciting sex. The apple in the garden of Eden was red."
Her look said *so there*.

"How do you know it was red? Maybe it was a
Granny Smith?"

"What woman would forfeit eternity for a Granny
Smith?"

"Maybe it was a Gala," another woman offered.

"I'd believe a Gala before I'd believe a Granny Smith.
At least they're sweet, and they're red."

"They're a pale, washed-out red."

"Girls, girls," Lolly chimed in as she perched on the
arm of an overstuffed, plastic-wrapped chair. "I'm sure
Holly doesn't want to hear us debate the merits of apples."

"Actually, it's sort of fascinating." Holly had never
had real friends of her own—she and her mother had
moved too much and later, when she'd been stuck in the
same city in foster care, she'd still gone from family to
family. She'd always wanted to join in on the conversa-
tions in the girls' locker room or at lunch, but she'd
learned early on to hold back.

Getting too friendly only made leaving that much
harder.

Not anymore.

"You're sweet. Isn't she sweet, girls?" A dozen heads
bobbed in agreement. "I know you've got bigger things
to worry over. Moving from a new town has got to be
exhausting."

"It's not that bad."

"Good, because the girls and I were hoping you could
make time to attend our monthly luncheon. It's always
the third Tuesday and we have some really great speak-

ers. We're primarily focused on topics that appeal to single women."

"Namely men," one of the other women chimed in.

"Definitely men."

"How to find them. How to keep them. How to please them. That's where you come in."

"I'm not sure I'm following you—" Holly started, her words lost as Lolly linked arms with her.

"Why, where are my manners? You don't just hand over a gift and then talk a woman's ear off. You have to open it!" She ushered Holly over to the sofa.

The two women on the sofa scooted apart and patted the spot between them. Holly adjusted her grip on the heavy box as she found herself steered into the spot between them.

"Go on," one woman said.

"Open it," came another encouragement.

With a dozen interested gazes hooked on her, she pulled off the bow and tore off the wrapping paper. She eyed the colorful patchwork quilt nestled in white tissue paper and a memory pulled at her.

She'd been in the second grade, sitting in the back of Mrs. Klatt's room, watching the entire class sing happy birthday to one of the other students. A girl with long blond hair and pink Barbie boots. The most popular girl at Chicago's Wallaby Elementary. Mrs. Klatt had presented the girl with a cupcake sporting a blazing pink candle while the kids had piled dozens of handmade gifts onto her desk. It was a tradition repeated for every student in Mrs. Klatt's class.

Everyone except Holly.

Her birthday came and went the following week, but there was no cupcake or candle or presents, or even a birthday song. Because Holly came and went herself, too fast for anyone to learn her birthday, much less remember it.

She blinked back the hot tears that sprang to her eyes. "It's really beautiful."

"Jennifer made it," Lolly said. "She sells them at her shop in town—Quilts and Stuff. She also sells the most divine candles…" The woman's voice faded as Holly's attention shifted back to the gift. Her fingers stroked the soft embroidery as she read the sentiment in bright pink stitch…

Home Sweet Home.

Something soft and warm unfolded inside of her, and she smiled.

"So you'll come then?" Lolly was saying. "To the luncheon?"

"I don't usually take time off during the week," she started. *Usually.* But Holly was doing away with her usual routine. She was starting fresh. Planting roots. Making friends. "I'd love to be there."

"Wonderful," Lolly said as she pushed to her feet.

"We can really use your help," Jennifer told her. "Your grandmother was the guru when it came to pleasing men and heaven knows we need all the help we can get."

"That's right," another woman chimed in. "Charlene Singer—she's the resident sexpert—is always preaching the same old, same old about inner beauty and emotional attraction and clicking on a psychological wavelength, but she doesn't give us anything really solid to work with."

"Like positions," one of the women chimed in.

"And techniques," another offered as they all moved toward the doorway.

"We think it's so cool that you're continuing the family tradition," Lolly told her as she pulled open the front door. "Why, when we heard you specialized in ultimate orgasms, I activated the phone tree right away. Every Juliet in the county knows you're here and they'll be thrilled to hear that you're going to speak."

"Speak? But I thought it was a luncheon?"

"You're the luncheon speaker." Lolly beamed. "It'll be our most informative meeting yet. It's about time the women in this town learned how to really please a man."

"But I cook for a living."

"That's what we're counting on."

"But—" Holly started, only to bite back the rest of her protest when Lolly turned expectant eyes on her. Holly's hands tightened on the soft quilt. "But I'll need some time to prepare." Okay, that wasn't the *no cotton-picking way* she'd intended, but she couldn't very well be rude. They'd come all this way outside of town and brought her a really great present and they were so nice.

"The luncheon isn't for three weeks. We meet at the community center off of Main Street. Cookie does the decorations, Jennifer provides the linens and we have the food catered in. This month is barbecued venison, so don't wear anything light-colored. Last time, Jill Marie Smith wore shell-pink. She's still trying to get the stains out of her lap. We'll see you then," Lolly rushed on. "And before then, I'm sure. It's such a small town."

"But—" Holly started again. The protest fell on deaf

ears as she found herself passed from one woman to the
next in a series of loose, informal hugs before the door
slammed quickly shut.

As she stood in the center of her living room, the quilt
in her hands, and tried to catch her breath, the truth of
what she'd just done came barreling at her like a semi
with bad brakes.

A luncheon speech. About pleasing a man.

A luncheon *speech*. About *pleasing a man*.

First off, the closest she'd ever come to a speech had
been a ninth grade book report at school number eight.
But that had been different. It didn't matter that she'd
had to read verbatim from her paper or that some of the
kids had snickered when she'd mispronounced tyranno-
saurus because she'd known there would be another
science class down the road, and she'd been right. Five
months later, she'd changed schools again, and families.

But this… This was different.

This was *home*.

Home Sweet Home.

As for the man-pleasing part… The only person she
usually pleased was herself—with a scrumptious dessert or an intense session with her favorite vibrator.

Up until Friday night, that is. She'd pleased Josh and
he'd certainly pleased her, but there'd been no formula to
it. It had just happened. She was a baker, for heaven's sake.

But the Juliets didn't seem to realize that. She was
Rose Farraday's granddaughter and, therefore, a chip off
the old block when it came to men and pleasure. Add-
ing to the misconception was the fact that she did profit
from sex, what with the sensual nature of her desserts.

She had to set them straight.

That's what she told herself when the doorbell rang a few minutes later. *Just open your mouth and set the record straight.*

She reached for the doorknob.

4

"I CAN'T TALK about how to please a man," Holly said as she opened the door.

"No problem." Sue—from the saloon on Friday night—stood on the front porch. "I'm really good at following written directions." The woman wore an old Texas Rangers jersey, tan shorts and flip-flops. Her hair had been pulled back in a ponytail. Her eyes looked red-rimmed. Dark shadows puddled beneath, as if she'd tossed and turned all night. And cried. She'd definitely been up crying.

Concern welled inside Holly and her own anxiety fled. "I'm really sorry. I thought you were one of the Juliets."

"I guess I am now. I *am* single." Sue tried to smile but the expression didn't quite touch her eyes. "I don't mean to barge in on you, but I had to say thanks. It was really nice of you to see me home on Friday night."

"Glad I could help. I know you're hurting right now, but things will get better. Especially if you try to stay busy. Find a way to occupy your free time."

Holly knew that firsthand because she'd done so after the breakup of her only romantic relationship. She'd thrown herself into school after breaking up with Don whom she'd dated a whopping four months during her first year in college.

She'd approached the situation with reservations because she'd always made it a habit of keeping her distance when it came to any type of relationship. But Don had been so sweet and she'd been so vulnerable. She'd never had a real boyfriend and the temptation was too much to resist since she knew she wouldn't be picking up and leaving anytime soon—she was only a freshman on a full academic scholarship to the University of Houston. She hadn't counted on the fact that Don would party too much, flunk out of school and be forced to return to his home in Alabama.

She'd been so hurt, she'd eaten her way through an entire bowl of fudge batter—chocolate helped sate her lustful cravings, but fudge soothed any hurt. She'd also cried and wallowed in her self-pity, but then she'd picked herself back up and focused on her life. On beefing up her defenses and moving on.

Her gaze went to Sue's red-rimmed eyes and her uncertain expression, and Holly's chest tightened. She'd only been in like with Don. She couldn't imagine the hurt if she'd let herself fall in love with him.

"You should definitely keep busy," Holly went on.

"I'm glad you said that because I have something to ask you." The woman pulled back her shoulders and lifted her chin as if to summon her courage. "I want to work for you." Before Holly could reply, she rushed on, "I'm single and I hate it, and the only way to change it is to make some changes." Uncertainty flashed in her gaze before she seemed to gather her confidence. She squared her shoulders again. "I'm going to turn myself into a sex kitten and lure my Bert Wayne back home. I figure I'll have to work on my looks and go on a diet. While I'm doing that, I want to beef up my know-how when it comes to pleasing my man. I know the nuts and bolts, of course. It's not like I'm a virgin or anything. But I was hoping you could teach me the extras."

"Me?"

"You're an expert."

"I'm afraid the only thing I can teach you is the difference between whisking and beating."

Sue seemed to think for a second. "I've never really been into any sort of bondage, but I guess I could give it a try. And I'll work really hard. I won't even take a lunch break. I'll be so dedicated you won't regret giving me this chance. I swear."

"I'm not in the pleasure business," Holly said, determined to set the record straight before she found herself committed to private lessons in addition to a speech on the subject. "I mean, I am. I please the taste buds. I don't please men."

"But the word around town is that you give the best orgasms around."

"I don't give orgasms. I make them."

"I know. That's why I'm here."

"I make them in my kitchen." She motioned Sue inside and led her into the kitchen. Picking up a mouthwatering confection, she turned to the woman. "Meet my Ultimate White Chocolate Orgasm, also available in milk chocolate."

"It's a dessert."

"Not just any dessert. It's a dessert for lovers. An aphrodisiac dessert meant to tantalize your taste buds and spice up your love life. So you see, while I am in the sex business, I'm not in the sexual *act* business. What I do is not nearly as exciting." She eyed Sue, noting the woman's suddenly bright eyes and trembling lips, as if Holly had snatched away her last hope.

"But I could use some help," Holly heard herself say. "I had a full-time baking assistant back in Houston. I haven't had a chance to post any want ads for some kitchen help, but I'm definitely hiring. If you're interested."

"I won't get to sleep with anyone?"

"Not during working hours."

"And I won't get to learn all those fancy hand job techniques that supposedly make a man beg for more?"

"The only thing your hands will be doing is running a mixer and pouring ingredients. But I do offer a nice dental plan and decent health insurance."

"Paid vacation?"

"One week after the first six months. And you get all the free desserts you can eat."

Sue eyed the various goodies spread out on the massive table. "Aphrodisiac, you say?" At Holly's nod, she added, "Well, it does hint at sex. Sort of." She shrugged. "I guess making sexy desserts could be almost as sexy as selling my body." She inhaled, her nostrils flaring at the scent of chocolate that filled the air, and a grin tugged at her lips. "You know, I actually do feel sexy."

"The smell of chocolate releases pheromones in the brain that trigger a sense of well-being."

She inhaled again and her expression turned into a

full-blown smile. "This turning over a new leaf is going to work, I just know it. Bert will be begging to come back in no time." She rubbed her hands together and glanced around. "Where do I start?"

"You follow this recipe and start a batch of Ooey Gooey Ecstasy in mixer number two." Holly handed her a folded apron from a nearby countertop and a pair of gloves. "The pecans and ginseng are in that cabinet over there. The rest of the stuff I have laid out on the countertop. I'm going to head to town and pick up some emergency bags of flour at the Food-o-rama to tide us over until the UPS guy comes."

"You might want to buy out the store. I saw Duke's truck go by here when I pulled in the driveway. He's the UPS contractor for this area. FedEx, too. He makes all the deliveries and judging by the direction he was heading, I don't think you'll get yours until sunset, at the earliest."

"But it's supposed to be delivered by noon."

"Yeah, well, Duke isn't one for following the rules when it comes to outsiders. Marge Jacoby moved back here from Centerville last year and waited damned near six months before she started getting her Home Shopping Club orders when she was supposed to."

"Is she getting them on time now?"

Sue smiled. "Now that you're here and someone's taken her place as the resident outsider. But don't worry. When someone else moves in to town, you'll be out of the hot seat."

"In six months."

"Or longer. We don't exactly have a population spurt going on right now."

Holly shook her head. "I am so screwed."

Sue shrugged. "Come now, things could be worse. The Food-o-rama could be closing early today like they do on Mondays, on account of Wilson Jamison—the owner—is the head moose over at the lodge and Monday is poker night."

"It *is* Monday."

"Oh." Sue shrugged. "I guess you really are screwed then."

HOLLY PULLED into the parking lot of Romeo's only grocery store five minutes before closing time and let loose a sigh of relief.

The Food-o-rama was a medium-size building located on the corner of the only significant intersection in town. It looked fairly new, with a paved parking lot, a shiny glass storefront and a huge sign with the name Food-o-rama in red script letters. The entire place would probably fit into the customer service department of a Wal-Mart Supercenter, but in the small town of Romeo, it seemed massive compared to the small businesses that lined nearby Main Street.

Climbing from her SUV, Holly snatched up her purse and rushed into the store. She grabbed a basket, dodged her way past several shoppers and found the flour with three minutes to spare.

Six bags languished on the shelf next to several empty rows.

Six? Six bags wouldn't get her through the order from Timmons Caterers, much less a full day's production.

Frustration started to well, but she quickly tamped it

back down. She could deal with this. Surely, Duke would make the delivery before dark. She could work through the night thereafter. She normally shipped out her desserts on Monday, Wednesday and Friday. But she could adjust her schedule and ship early tomorrow morning. Duke didn't do refrigerated items and so she'd found a shipping center in nearby Cherryville that could ship out her desserts. As for supplies…she'd anticipated having them sent directly to her house but she might have to rethink that plan and pick up her shipments in Cherryville if Duke didn't come through in the future.

But she intended to give him a chance first and, in the meantime, make due with the six available bags… Make that five.

Her mouth dropped open as a thin, frail arm reached past her and snagged one of the bags.

She turned to see a small, fragile-looking woman with snow-white hair, a rose-printed dress and white patent leather pumps.

"Wait," Holly blurted as the woman set the flour in her cart. "I really need that."

"I beg your pardon, dear?" She reached for another bag.

"I'm a professional baker and I haven't got my shipment of flour."

"What a small world. Why, I'm a baker, too, of sorts. I mainly brew tea right now, but I've decided to try my hand at making some homemade scones to go with my special recipe Earl Grey." She snagged a second bag of flour before Holly could protest. "There's nothing like homemade scones to make a person extra thirsty. Say—" She adjusted the thick bifocals that perched on the tip of her nose and fastened around her neck via a shiny gold chain. "You wouldn't be that there baker who's set up shop out at Rose's place?"

"You've heard about me?"

"It's a small town, dear."

"I mean, of course, you've heard about me. But you obviously heard the truth."

"That's because I listen with both ears instead of just hearing the juicy parts. I've never been one for gossip. Gossip poisons people, that's what my Lester used to say." Sadness flashed in her eyes before she managed another smile. "He was never much for gossip, either, which is why we fit like two peas in a pod. Or we used to until he passed on about five years back."

"I'm so sorry."

"Don't be, child." She patted Holly's arm. "We had a lot of years together. And shared a lot of tea. He always loved my tea, and so I opened up shop a few years back and what do you know? Half the town loves my stuff, too. I'm Martha Reynolds." She held out her hand. "I own Miss Martha's Tearoom over by the courthouse."

"Holly Farraday. I own Sweet & Sinful. My business is primarily Web-based, so I work out of my home."

"The Farraday Inn?"

"Rose left it to me. She was my grandmother."

"Of course she was, child. Why, you're the spitting image of her."

"You knew her?"

"Everyone in town knew Rose. So you've turned the Farraday Inn into a bona fide bakery, have you?"

"Yes, ma'am." Her gaze dropped to the flour in Miss Martha's cart. "I'd be willing to pay you for those bags."

"But I haven't bought them yet."

"Then I'd be willing to pay you not to buy them."

The woman smiled, her face scrunching into a mass of wrinkles. Her pale blue eyes lit with amusement. "What if you can't afford me?"

"How much are you asking?"

She seemed to think for a moment. "A free dessert?"

"I'll make it two."

"I s'pose I could just pick up a package of tea cookies on the next aisle and try my hand at baking some other time."

"My treat."

"In that case, I think these are yours." She handed over the flour and led Holly over to the cookie aisle.

Minutes later, Holly stood in front of the Food-o-rama, handed over the two boxes of Danish Butter Cookies she'd purchased and thanked Miss Martha again.

"Don't be silly, child. In this town, we business owners stick together. Speaking of which, the Romeo chamber of commerce meets every Monday night and sometimes Friday afternoons. You might consider stopping by and introducing yourself. We handle the occasional business matter—field complaints from citizens and the like—but mostly we work on various charity projects. We're organizing a school clothing drive for some of the needy families in the area. It's a good way to meet people and get involved in the community."

"I'm really very busy," Holly started to say before she caught herself.

She *was* busy, which had always been a good excuse to keep to herself. She'd been too busy doing homework to stay after for cheerleader tryouts in the seventh grade at one of the three intermediate schools she'd attended. And she'd been too busy preparing for her SATs to attend her junior year prom with Marshall LaFoy, a pimply-faced boy who'd had a crush on her the eight months she'd been a student at Harborstown High School on Chicago's East Side neighborhood. And she'd been too busy working a part-time job at the Diamond Bakery to join the senior girls' club or attend any of the numerous graduation parties the spring she'd turned eighteen, graduated from Washington High School and left the foster care system for good.

She was always busy.

But things were different now. *She* was different. Or she would be just as soon as she stopped keeping her distance from everyone and everything and actually settled in for the long haul.

"I'll be there," she told Miss Martha. "And thanks again. I'll get your desserts to you as soon as possible."

"No hurry, child. I'm not going anywhere."

Neither am I, Holly thought and smiled to herself as she walked to her Navigator to head back to the Farraday Inn. *Neither am I.*

JOSH WAS GOING straight to hell. *No stops or detours.*

The notion rooted in his head as he stood outside the feed store and watched Holly Farraday load her grocery bags into the back of her Lincoln Navigator. *Hell* because the only thing he thought of when he looked at her was the way she'd felt and tasted when he'd kissed her.

He hadn't given the property a second thought, much less brainstormed any persuasive means to get her to sell.

It seemed he didn't want the land half as much as he wanted to slide into her hot, sweet little body.

The trouble was, sex would only sate the lust burning him up from the inside out. It wouldn't do a damned thing for his conscience.

He watched the Navigator as it pulled out of the parking lot and disappeared up the road. The minute she was out of sight, he realized he'd been holding his breath. He blew out an exasperated sigh and drank in enough oxygen to jump-start his common sense.

What was he doing?

He was a grown man, not some horny teenager who couldn't keep from staring or lusting or hurting at the sight of a woman. He had maturity on his side. Experience. Wisdom.

A bona fide hard-on pushing tight against the zipper of his jeans.

"Dammit," he muttered, forcing his attention to the large pile of feed sacks sitting on the curb beside his truck. He yanked the tailgate down and hoisted the first sack into the truck bed. He had a pile of work waiting for him. He didn't have time for this, for her, and so he vowed not to even spare a glance at her place when he passed by a few hours later after finishing his errands in town.

Instead, he made a mental list of all the chores he had waiting, the phone calls he'd yet to make, the meetings he needed to attend. What with all the responsibilities that came with running the biggest horse ranch in the state, he barely had time to breathe, let alone think. Fantasize. *Wonder.*

If another long, slow lick of Holly Farraday would taste half as good as the first.

The fading white farmhouse caught the corner of his eye, and he couldn't seem to help himself. He turned and caught a glimpse of her as she passed in front of the kitchen window. His gut tightened and his stomach hollowed out, and he knew.

She would taste even better. Richer. Sweeter. More sinful.

The knowledge haunted him all the way back to the ranch where he unloaded the feed and checked on several of the mares scheduled for breeding in the coming week. The Iron Horse ran cattle for the most part, but they also bred some of the finest cutting horses in the country. While Josh had been away from the ranch over fifteen years, it didn't make him any less capable. He'd lived and breathed the ranch like his father and grandfather before him while growing up and so he fell into his old role as if he'd never left.

As if it were his destiny.

Josh pushed away the thought and focused his attention on saddling his horse. He spent the next several hours rounding up strays on the back forty until his muscles ached and exhaustion tugged at him, but he didn't stop. He couldn't. Not until he was too tired to do anything but fall into a deep sleep.

By the time Josh rode back into the barn and unsaddled his horse, it was well after dark. The only light came from the inside of the barn and the full moon that shimmered overhead. All of the ranch hands had long since left or retired to the bunkhouse where several bedded down during the week to avoid the long drive to and from town.

He hooked his saddle on the wall, brushed his horse down and walked toward the house that sat on the horizon. The ranch house was a sprawling one-story structure made of rock and stained wood. A massive front porch spanned from side to side. Wooden ceiling fans swirled from the high ceiling, stirring a small breeze that offered little relief from the sweltering heat.

Lights blazed inside the house and the sound of voices drifted from the kitchen where his great-uncle Eustace and great-aunt Lurline argued over supper.

"But I wanted biscuits," Eustace told her.

"We always have biscuits. I thought cornbread would be a nice change."

"That's the trouble with you, Lurline. You think too much."

"Obviously I don't think enough, otherwise I never would have married the likes of you...."

Josh thought about joining them, but he wasn't in the mood to play referee. Not that it would help matters. They lived to argue. Hell, he had a hunch they liked to argue given the amount of time they devoted to the task and so he'd learned to keep his mouth shut over the past few months.

He headed straight into the shower.

The minute the warm liquid slid over his aching muscles, he closed his eyes and relished the sensation. Steam rushed from the hot water and a fog quickly surrounded him. He drew in a deep breath, eager for the fog to fill his brain while the water pelted his skin.

The hotter, the better.

Just as the thought registered, an image appeared in his mind. Holly. Right there in front of him. Naked and slick and hot—

His eyes popped open and he stared down. His dick bobbed with excitement and he swore.

There would be no Holly. No *naked* or *slick* or *hot.* Sex wasn't a possibility because Holly Farraday didn't want a good roll in the hay. She wanted a *relationship,* and Josh had sworn off those years ago.

The knowledge should have been enough to push her out of his fantasies and into the *Hands Off* section of his mind. Christ, it had always been enough because Josh knew from watching every other McGraw man before him that he simply wasn't the marrying kind. The faithful kind. The type of man who could love a woman enough to make a lifelong commitment and mean it.

Till death do us part.

Josh didn't believe in the concept of romantic love. In all his thirty-four years, he'd never felt such a thing, and he sure-as-shootin' had never seen it firsthand. And so, in his opinion, no such thing existed.

But lust… Now that was all too real and powerful, and more than enough to keep Josh McGraw wide-awake and wanting for the rest of the night.

5

HOLLY STIFLED a yawn and pulled another stack of ledgers from the old chest she'd been rummaging through. It was well after midnight and she would normally be asleep at this time. But she still hadn't given up on Duke. While she'd waited, she'd decided to tackle the upstairs.

She hadn't realized the enormity of her inheritance until she'd actually walked through the house, room to room, and realized the work ahead of her. There were knickknacks to pack away and closets to go through as she made her way through each room and decided what to keep and what to toss. She didn't even want to think about the overgrown acres that surrounded the huge house.

One thing at a time, she'd told herself.

House tonight. Yard tomorrow.

Her grandmother's room had been the obvious starting point since Holly had decided to use the bedroom as her own. She'd targeted the three old cedar chests that stood stacked in the far corner. Clearing them out would make room for her own belongings which still sat in boxes in the living room.

The first chest contained her grandmother's business

records. The woman had kept not only a list of every transaction, but every client, as well. From her premium customers—the men who frequented more than once a week—to her Friday night regulars, to the special occasion Joes—the men who visited on various holidays and birthdays. She kept a detailed record of who not only came and went, but who *came,* and went. Each name was followed by an *O* for orgasm, followed by the name of the woman he'd kept company with, followed by an *O,* as well. While the majority of men came, Holly was surprised to find that the experience had been mutually satisfying for the women.

In addition to the extensive record keeping, her grandmother had kept all the appropriate financials, from profit-and-loss statements to accounts receivable. At first, it had seemed silly to Holly for her grandmother to keep such conventional documents for such an unconventional business. But the more she leafed through the various statements, including IRS forms listing the inn as a "restaurant," she realized that the income had been too large to simply tuck away in a cookie jar. Back in the late forties, there had been few, if any, occupations for women that paid in a year what the Farraday Inn grossed on a weekly basis. Rose, however, hadn't reaped the reward alone. She'd divided the earnings up equally between herself and her girls.

It seemed that Rose Farraday had been generous, as well as beautiful.

She'd also been creative.

Holly came to that conclusion when she unearthed the spiral notebook from the bottom of the trunk.

Holly's heart kicked up a beat as she thumbed through the pages and realized her find. Her grandmother's recipe book.

Her gaze scanned the first section entitled *Appeteasers,* which detailed step-by-step specifics for such delicacies as *Stirring Cinnamon Dip, Sweet Honey Nips, Brandy Kisses* and *Southern Cider.* The main entrées—listed as main *entries*—section included recipes for everything from *Rose's Back-Porch Barbecue* to her *Hot Doggy Delight.*

Holly wanted to laugh. At the same time, her heart pounded and her blood rushed at an alarming rate. While the menu seemed almost cheesy now, back in its day it had been Rose's ticket to sexual success. The key to dozens of satisfied men. Tried and true ways to tease and please any and every man.

The Juliets would go nuts for Rose's recipes.

Provided they still worked every bit as well as they had fifty years ago. Probably. Maybe. Times had certainly changed. There was only one way to guarantee success—by trying out the recipes firsthand with Josh McGraw.

The minute the notion struck, heat flowered in her belly and her lips tingled.

Sure, she'd sworn off men like Josh—the here today, gone tomorrow type—when it came to relationships. But this wouldn't be a relationship. It would be a business proposition, and the ideal way to work him out of her system. *That,* she needed more than anything.

Holly couldn't stop thinking about Friday night because she'd had such an incredible orgasm. But she'd been coming off a major dry spell and so any orgasm with a man would *seem* incredible. It wasn't that Josh affected her in a way unlike any other man. She knew that, but to really believe it, she needed to have sex with him again.

She savored the thought for a long moment before tucking it aside and turning her attention back to the chest. *One thing at a time.*

The house. The yard. Then Josh McGraw.

"How much?" Holly's gaze ping-ponged between the bright green-and-yellow machine and the owner of Romeo's only hardware store. Before the man could re-cite the outrageous price listed on the tag hanging from the steering wheel, she shook her head. "No way am I paying eight thousand dollars for a lawn mower."

Sure, her land was overgrown and the only thing she'd found in the old barn had been a small push mower that wouldn't even start and she'd planned to start her garden today after cutting the grass. But *thousands* of dollars? For a *lawn mower?*

"This, little lady, is a John Deere Deluxe Tractor, Model 980, the latest and most advanced system in land maintenance and cultivation," explained Arlee Summers, the sixty-something man who'd met her at the door the minute she'd walked into Romeo's only hardware store. He wore red overalls embroidered with Arlee's Hardware & Feed in large yellow letters across the back. He had snow-white hair, pale blue eyes and a patient smile that said he was an old pro at dealing with disbelievers. "It comes complete with a mulch package, a fertilizer carrier and a five-blade expansion system. It's also got a V6 engine, a hydraulic clutch and transmission and a state-of-the-art aluminum carburetor construction." He stroked the hood reverently. "This filly's as fast as they come."

"I'm going to cut grass, not enter the Daytona 500." Her lips drew into a frown. If he thought he had a sucker standing in front of him, he had another thing coming. She was a businesswoman, for heaven's sake. A very successful businesswoman with one of the fastest-growing companies on the Internet. "It's a *lawn mower*," she said in her best you-have-to-be-kidding tone.

"It's got cup holders and a retractable awning."

"I'll take it." Hey, she was a very successful businesswoman with one of the fastest-growing companies on the Internet and fifty acres of grass to mow *and* this was Texas. As in hot. As in *hot*.

Arlee smiled and pulled the tag from the tractor. "I'll ring you up and have her delivered out to your place."

"You do drive a hard bargain." The deep voice slid into her ears and sent heat thrumming along her nerve endings. She drew a steady breath and turned to find Josh McGraw standing behind her. His blue eyes twinkled and a smile curved his full lips.

Holly tried to ignore the sudden flutter in her chest. She shrugged. "What can I say? The thought of collapsing from exposure or dehydration scares the daylights out of me."

His smile faded. "It should. This isn't the city with its nice, neat little neighborhoods and pretty flower gardens. You're way out of your element now." His gaze did a slow trek from her halter top and capri pants, to her strappy sandals—she still hadn't managed to unearth her boots and jeans. "Taking care of a spread the size of yours would be hard and time-consuming for someone who grew up around here. You're in over your head, even with an eight-thousand-dollar lawn mower."

"It's a tractor," she corrected. "And thanks for the vote of confidence. How soon did you say you could deliver it?"

Arlee smiled. "I'll have my delivery boy follow you out to your place right now."

TWO HOURS LATER, Holly slid on her sunglasses, set her water bottle in the deluxe drink holder and climbed onto the tractor. The awning shielded the top of her head from the sun's brutal rays and made the heat somewhat bearable.

For about the time it took to start the tractor.

Sweat streamed down her face as she fought with the steering wheel and tried to keep the machine eating grass in a straight line.

Metal ground against rock and the tractor jumped. The front wheels took a sharp turn to the left. Holly grappled for the steering wheel. Her damp palms slid over the vinyl and rubbed her skin raw.

In less than fifteen minutes, she'd developed a new-found respect for lawn maintenance workers. Sure, it was hot in her kitchen, but she didn't have to fight with an oven that seemed hell-bent on not working properly.

"Come on, Green Machine," she pleaded. "Cooperate."

The Green Machine obviously didn't come with ears even though the price had been outrageous. She hit more rocks as she bounced along, ran over a protruding tree stump and knocked over the Welcome to the Farraday Inn sign that had sat in the yard for five decades.

"Way to go," she told herself. "Forget getting to know your past. Just plow right over it."

Her arms ached as she gripped the steering wheel and rounded the edge of the yard. She approached the small grassless area off to the far right that had once been a garden. Weeds grew over the edges of the white wire that outlined the space. She knew she wouldn't be able to cut all of the overgrowth, but the goal was to get as close as possible. She could pull the rest of the weeds by hand when she planted the flowers she'd picked up in town.

"Relax," she told herself as she cut a sharp corner just shy of the white wire that sealed off the area. "You can do this. Just skim the edges and don't get too close."

The thought echoed just as one of the blades struck metal and sucked up part of the wire edging. Holly kept going, determined to get back on track and get busy. But it never quite happened.

After a full hour, she'd barely finished cutting near the garden. Forget the acres and acres of overgrown grass that stretched endlessly on the other side of the white wicker fence to a far-off grove of trees.

"Are you done yet?" Sue asked as she stepped down off the porch filled with the flowers Holly had picked up at the nursery. Her sandal caught in a ball of mangled wire and she fought to get free.

"Not quite," Holly said. "I think I'll ask around town and see if I can get some yard help."

"Good idea." Sue extracted her shoe from the wire and held it up. "I'll spread the word for you."

WHILE CUTTING the grass hadn't gone as planned, Holly was still determined to get on with her garden. With her how-to book in hand—she'd never actually planted a garden before—she weeded the area and started digging her holes. She spent the next several hours transferring the flowers from pot to ground. When she'd finally patted the last bit of dirt back into place, she leaned back on her haunches and surveyed her work.

Color brightened the otherwise drab area and she smiled. While the day hadn't gone exactly as planned, she had made some progress.

She dusted off her hands and headed for the water spout on the side of the house. She was busy washing the dirt from her hands when she heard the deep voice.

"You should consider my offer."

She glanced up to see Josh standing behind her. Her gaze met his and she licked her suddenly dry lips. Her heart stalled and she felt the familiar pull between her legs. Where she'd had her doubts when the outrageous idea had first struck back in her grandmother's room, her hesitation quickly surrendered to the need building inside her.

"Actually," she told him, "you should consider mine."

Surprise registered on his face and his eyebrows hitched together. "What offer?"

She licked her lips again and tried to control the sudden pounding of her heart. "The one I'm about to make."

"LET ME GET this straight." Josh drew a deep breath and leveled a stare at the woman sitting across the kitchen table from him. Sue had already left for the day and they were alone. The sweet scent of cupcakes drifted from across the table where she sat sipping a Diet Coke. "If I try out your grandmother's recipes with you, you'll sell me your land."

"Not all of the recipes, just her most popular items. And I'm not offering all of my land, just half. Twenty-five acres. If you agree, I'll have Mike draw up the transfer papers this afternoon."

"You're really serious?"

"As serious as a tablespoon of pure vanilla extract."

He ran a hand over his face and eyed her. "I don't believe this."

"What's not to believe? You've got something I want, and I've got something you want. It's good business."

"It's sex."

"It's research sex. I can't very well share my grandmother's recipes without trying them out first. I sample every batch of my desserts for taste and consistency and overall quality. I never pass on a product unless I know it's wonderful. Likewise, I can't just pass on a bunch of outdated techniques unless I know they really work."

He couldn't help but admire her integrity, a fact that surprised the hell out of him because Josh's admiration rarely extended beyond a nice ass or a gorgeous pair of legs. "Why me?"

"Because I have something you want," she said, "and we have great chemistry." Her gaze met his and he knew she was thinking of their explosive one-night stand. "I need to know firsthand what made the Farraday Inn so wildly popular. Who better to do it with than someone I'm attracted to? Not to mention, you're perfect. You're temporary."

"Which means you won't have to face me the morning after."

"Exactly. It's perfect."

He'd been thinking the exact same thing, but there was just something about hearing her say it that made him feel almost angry. As if he wasn't good enough for more in her eyes.

As if he wanted to be.

Josh dismissed the ridiculous thought. This was a dream come true. Christ, he'd been fantasizing about her for the past few days and here was his chance to turn those fantasies into real life.

"I know twenty-five acres isn't what you had in mind, but it's the best I can offer."

"When do we start?"

"The speech is in three weeks. I've figured out that it will take us five encounters to try out all eight recipes— the first four are 'appeteasers' and we can do those together. Since I'm busy during the week and I'm sure you are, too, the only free time I have is on the weekend. I was thinking we could start tonight and then do both Friday and Saturday for the next two weekends. That makes five."

"Tonight?"

She smiled then, her full, slick lips parting, and he swallowed. "Seven o'clock sharp."

6

HOLLY HAD FANTASIZED about kissing Josh again, even before she'd come up with the brilliant idea to beef up her orgasmic experience by sampling every offering on "The Menu of Sexual Delights." Since their first night together, she'd thought of him much too often for her own peace of mind. The enticing scent of him filling her nostrils. The warmth of his skin beneath her fingertips. The delicious taste of his lips. The bold thrust of his tongue.

But the fantasy couldn't begin to compare to the real man. He smelled even better, felt even hotter, tasted even sweeter, and he gave new meaning to the word *bold* as he toed the door closed with the tip of his boot later that night, backed her into the room and pressed her up against the nearest wall.

The kiss that followed had her panting and clawing at his shoulders before she realized that neither were on the coveted menu. At least not this soon.

"Wait," she managed, tearing her lips from his. "It's not supposed to be like this." When he gave her a knowing look, she added, "I mean, it is supposed to be like this—passionate and intense—but not like *this*."

She pulled away from him and took his hands in hers, leading him toward the sofa. "Your table is ready and waiting. I'll be your server tonight." She urged him into a chair. "Have a look and I'll be right back to take your order."

Holly left Josh to go over the menu while she retreated into the kitchen. She drew a deep breath. Her nipples pressed tight against her blouse. The material rubbed the ripe tips and a gasp burst past her lips. The intense reaction startled her. She'd never responded so fiercely to a man before. Then again, it was that fact that had prompted her to proposition him in the first place.

He was hot. Sensual. Stimulating.

And ready to order.

The sound of the bell echoed in her ear and sent a bolt of adrenaline through her. She stiffened and tried to calm her suddenly pounding heart. As quickly as she could, she stripped down her to her bra and panties. Her fingers stalled just an inch shy of her bra closure and doubt bolted through her. A crazy sensation. She'd already made up her mind to follow the menu. Besides, as nervous as the thought of parading naked in front of Josh McGraw made her, it made her equally excited.

She forced her fingers into action until she'd shed her clothes and donned the uniform worn by the women of the Farraday Inn. Then she drew a deep breath and pushed through the kitchen door.

JOSH DREW IN a deep breath and tried to slow the fierce pounding of his heart. He had to get a grip if he intended to make even one of the menu selections without coming in his pants.

A definite possibility, he realized as he read the suggestive offerings. Each conjured an image that made it harder to breathe. Hard, period.

He wanted to slide into her warm, luscious body over and over again until he stopped thinking about her.

She had him by the short hairs, hot and panting like some wet-behind-the-ears kid. But that was going to change. Before it was all said and done, Josh intended to get his fill of Holly Farraday. Then she would become just another woman in his past. Nobody special. Nobody who could keep him up all night with just the memory of her soft lips and hot tongue.

Josh McGraw didn't do special. He liked all women, and they liked him. He was plainspoken, highly sensual and only interested in one thing when it came to women. He knew it sounded cold, unfeeling, even. But the truth of the matter was Josh felt too much. Lust was a powerful thing and often misinterpreted for something deeper. But not by him. He wasn't continuing the grand McGraw tradition of lying and cheating on his partner.

He pushed away the strange sense of melancholy that crept through him and focused on the frantic beat of his heart. This wasn't about commitment. Not by a long shot. It was sex, pure and simple and uncomplicated, just the way Josh liked it.

"Pretty interesting, huh?" The soft sweet voice came from behind.

Josh turned to see Holly approach the table. His heart jammed into his throat and his stomach went hollow.

She wore nothing but a filmy black apron tied around her small waist and a matching bra. Her nipples were dark, inviting shadows beneath the lace. Her breasts were plumped and full and so close to spilling over the cups.

She looked soft and rounded in all the right places and the urge to grip her waist and pull her into his lap and onto his throbbing cock was damned near too much for him to handle.

He gripped the edge of the menu and forced his gaze back to the tantalizing list. "I first heard about this menu when I was a kid. It was more like a tall tale back then. Like the tooth fairy. Some believed it existed. Some didn't. But no one really *knew.* Then when I was in the ninth grade, this guy on the basketball team got his hands on one his father had swiped on a visit. It was the hot topic in the boys' locker room from then on."

"I didn't think boys gossiped."

He grinned. "We don't. We talk. Speculate." His gaze locked with hers and his expression went serious. "Fantasize."

The word seemed to dangle between them for several long seconds. The air that surrounded them grew thick and hot. Her gaze darkened and she licked her lips, and he knew she wanted him as much as he wanted her.

Not that he'd had any doubts. She'd propositioned him. Obviously she felt the same fierce need, even if she did seem to be doing a fine job of controlling herself.

"So how do you want to do this?" he finally asked.

Another swipe at her bottom lip and she drew a deep

breath. The action pushed her breasts up and out and need twisted his gut. "It seems the most practical to start at the top and work our way through one item at a time. At least, that's what I was thinking. The appeteasers are smaller items and don't require as much time, so we can do two at a time."

"Why not go for broke and do all four tonight?"

"We don't have enough time. I only scheduled two hours for this. I still have some things to do in my kitchen."

"I thought you took Saturday nights off."

"That was back in Houston. But since none of my shipments have come on time, I'm behind. I'll be working this weekend to try to catch up. Which means I have to be in my kitchen in two hours to prepare tomorrow's work schedule."

If there was one thing Josh had learned about Holly in the few short days she'd been in town, it was that she prided herself on following her coveted schedule.

He couldn't help but wonder as she turned to lead him upstairs what it would be like to see her off her schedule, acting on raw impulse rather than a step-by-step plan. He had the sudden impulse to yank her around, press her up against the nearest wall and take her right then and there the way he'd wanted to when she'd first opened the door to him a half hour ago.

But as much as he wanted to shake up Holly's world, he knew pushing her too far, too fast would likely get him booted out the front door. He'd meant what he'd said about the menu. Like every other freshman boy who'd seen the notorious menu up close and personal

in the locker room that time, he'd done his fair share of
fantasizing about the various sexual delicacies, and he
wasn't about to miss his chance to sample each one for
himself.

Josh gathered his control, gripped the banister and
followed her up the stairs.

HOLLY TOSSED the cinnamon sticks into the hot, steaming bathtub before turning to light the candles spread
throughout the large *Tease & Please* room, first room
at the top of the stairs which still contained the large
claw-foot tub used to serve up Rose's infamous Stirring
Cinnamon Dip—a warm, fragrant bath scented with
cinnamon and cloves. Guaranteed to relax and revive.
Her gaze slid over her shoulder to the man who stood
framed in the doorway, watching her.

Not that Josh McGraw needed to revive. Soft denim
strained over his growing bulge. He was revved and ready.

She knew the feeling.

The spicy scent teased her nostrils and made her
heart drum faster. She turned toward the small round
table that held a jar of honey and a bottle of aged liquor
for items two and three on the list—Sweet Honey Nips
and Brandy Kisses. Her mouth watered and her nipples
strained against the skimpy bra. With each of her movements, the lace rubbed and chafed and sent prickles of
awareness up and down her arms. Heat pulsed between
her legs and a steady ache gnawed at her belly. Her
gaze caught and held his and she licked her lips, tasting
him and suddenly wishing she hadn't stopped things
earlier with the silly menu.

But she meant to learn from the experience, and fast and furious was not conducive to her plan. It was all about taking things slow and thorough and proving beyond a doubt that the menu worked for both parties. It was about doing and documenting.

It wasn't about *feeling*.

She knew that, at the same time, she couldn't *not* feel. The drumming of her heart inside her chest. The moist steam from the tub bathing her face. The perspiration tickling its way down her neck.

Holly had been so focused on the grand finale and what it would feel like to climax with him that she hadn't anticipated the intensity of each small detail along the way, or how delicious the simple act of breathing could be, how exciting with Josh McGraw watching her.

"Dinner is served," she said, motioning to the tub.

She watched as he bent down and tugged off one boot then the other. His socks followed. He peeled his white T-shirt up and over his head. Her breath caught and held as he reached for the waistband of his jeans.

Strong, purposeful fingers slid the button free before tackling the zipper. The teeth parted. She glimpsed crisp white cotton briefs before he hooked his thumbs in the waistband and pushed the jeans and underwear down with one swift motion. Denim puddled around his ankles before he stepped free and kicked the clothing to the side.

She'd never been visual when it came to getting aroused. She'd never subscribed to a nude magazine or rented a porn flick. To Holly, words had always been her weakness. A good romance novel or an erotic short story never failed to put her into a sexy mindset. But the sight of Josh McGraw completely naked and fully erect made her rethink her position. Even the most explicit book had never made her mouth go dry or her hands shake. As for the intensity of the heat sweeping her from head to toe... Playgirl, *here I come*.

Her gaze traveled over him slowly, following the outline of his shoulders, his sinewy chest and narrow waist. A tattoo circled one muscled bicep. He looked fierce and rugged and very hungry as he stared back at her, his gaze dark and disturbing and...impatient. Yet he made no move forward and she realized that, despite the whirlwind of lust evident in his expression, he wasn't going to let it rage out of control.

Not yet.

She moved to the side and watched as he walked past her. He stepped into the tub and sank down into the steaming water. She walked to the cabinet and picked up her kitchen timer.

"What's that for?" he asked as she set the timer for two hours.

"To make sure we don't go over our scheduled time." She left the timer ticking away and walked back to the tub. She knelt by the edge and reached for the soap. Rolling the fragrant bar between her palms, she watched the lather build before she touched him.

Her breath hitched at the first feel of his warm skin beneath her hand. Desire knifed through her and she clamped her legs together, determined to calm the sudden ache that was pleasure and pain all rolled into the same package. She found herself wondering if the women who'd knelt in this spot countless times before her had felt the same intense arousal.

Maybe.

Probably.

While the inn had catered to a man's pleasure, Rose had made it clear in her records that her girls had enjoyed the delicacies just as much as the customers. That's why they'd all stayed with her for so long. They became addicted to the pleasure as much as the men who'd visited them time and time again.

Holly trailed her hands over his hard muscles and hair-roughened skin and felt her own hunger grow. She drew a deep, steady breath and concentrated on spreading the lather across his skin. She feathered her fingertips over his collarbone, swirled the soap around his nipples. The nubs grew hard beneath her touch and his breathing became more raspy.

Moving south, she traced the edge of his rib cage, palming her way down over his six-pack abs and stopping just shy of dipping beneath the water. The head of his erection bobbed just above the surface of the water. She touched the ripe purple head and his breathing seemed to stop. His body went taut and his gaze burned into her as if he waited to see what she would do next.

She touched him again, tracing the ridge before dipping her hand beneath the water and sliding her way down his shaft. She stroked him, up and down, twisting her fingers around and around. He seemed to grow harder in her hands, pulsing beneath her rhythmic touch. The heat from his shaft seeped into her palms. She felt his hand press between her shoulder blades and she glanced up into his smoldering gaze. Everything she felt whirling deep inside her—desire and need and excitement—reflected in his gaze. His fingertips burned into her skin and her own breath caught. Her lips parted as she tried to draw more air, but she couldn't seem to get enough to fill her lungs.

She licked her lips and forced her attention back to his erection. Before she could stroke him again, he caught her with his other hand. "Stop."

"It's part of the appeteaser. It works you up."

"I'm about as worked up as I'm going to get, cupcake."

When he let go of her hand, she almost squeezed him again, just to hear his deep, throaty growl of pure pleasure. She'd never been so eager to please a man before. The realization might have startled her if the circumstances had been different—if this had been a real date with a viable relationship prospect.

But her eagerness to please had nothing to do with the man himself and everything to do with the main event. It wasn't that she wanted to please *him*. She wanted to experience the ultimate orgasm, and working up Josh McGraw was just a necessary means to an end.

An end that wasn't going to come tonight. The appetizers were just that—teasers. Sexual delights to build anticipation so that the climax to come would not only be good, but out of this world.

She avoided his penis and dipped her hands beneath the water to cup his testicles. She rolled them, massaged and kneaded. She was just about to trace the inside of his thigh when he bent his leg and forced her upright.

"Enough. Let's move on to the next one."

"Sweet Honey Nips," she murmured as she retrieved the sticky sweetness and dribbled it onto his collarbone. Leaning down, she lapped at the golden river before trailing her tongue across his Adam's apple and up the side of his neck. She nibbled and licked at the sweet path before leaning back to drip-drop more onto his chest. She flicked her tongue over his nipple and he slid his arms around her, hauling her into his lap.

"My turn," he said, reaching for the honey. He dribbled it onto her breasts, watching as the liquid slid down her throat, over her breasts until a golden drop gathered on the tip of her ripe nipple. He lapped at the sweetness with his tongue, a hot fleck that brought a strangled moan from her throat.

"But I think I'm supposed to do this to you."

"I'm the customer and I want it served up my way."

She wanted to tell him that he was no such thing—they were equal partners in the agreement—but then he drew her deep into his mouth and suckled, and the words stalled in her throat. A sharp sensation tugged between her legs. She closed her eyes as the sensation built. He sucked harder and deeper and pushed her closer. This was it. She was going to go over the edge....

The realization sent a bolt of anxiety through her because she didn't want it like this—with nothing more than his mouth at her breast. She wanted the ultimate orgasm. The kind Rose had given her customers for nearly fifty years. The kind sure to win her the confidence and friendship of the Juliets.

"Wait," she gasped. "Not yet. Not like this."

"Kiss me," he told her, angling her head as he pulled her close.

"But I haven't drunk the brandy." She reached for the bottle, but he took it from her and took a long swig himself. "You shouldn't do that. Alcohol puts a damper on the male libido."

"I need all the help I can get, otherwise, we're not making it out of this bathroom by ten." And then he pulled her close and kissed her.

He tasted of warm brandy and hot man and the combination took her breath away. Where she'd meant to put the brakes on, the insistent thrust of his tongue only pushed her that much closer.

She lost herself for the next few moments. She slid her arms around his neck and plunged her tongue into his mouth to tangle with his. It wasn't until she felt his hand on her thigh that reason jumped to attention.

"I... We have to stop," she managed as she tore her mouth from his. "It'll be better if we wait."

"If it gets any better than this, you're going to be flat on your back and I'm going to be inside of you before you can spell the word *menu*."

His statement pleased her a lot more than it should have considering she didn't really care what Josh Mc-Graw thought. She didn't care, period.

This was business. Pure and simple. And he was temporary.

And delicious.

So very delicious, she decided as he plunged his tongue deep and took her breath away. He loved her with his mouth for what seemed an eternity, until she forgot all about the menu and gave herself over to the need clawing in her belly. She slid her arms around his neck and angled her head as the kiss deepened. His fingers slid up her thigh, trailing along the inside until he was so close to touching her. She shimmied, begging him the last few inches until he reached his destination. His fingertips slid over her damp flesh and... *There.* Right there—

Rrring...

The timer exploded and reality caved in on Holly. She went rigid, instantly aware of his hands and the fact that the appeteasers had made no mention of his hands down there, *in* there.

"I—" She swallowed. "It's over. We're finished."

"Cupcake, we're barely getting started." He pressed damp lips to the hollow of her throat and warmth unfolded in her chest.

The feeling was enough to galvanize her into action, because it had nothing to do with sex and everything to do with the fact that no man had ever kissed her quite so tenderly, with such conviction, and it touched her.

She pushed his hand away, wiggled from his grasp and scrambled from the tub. Distance would help. And not looking, she added as her gaze snagged on his strong, tanned body which overwhelmed the old-fashioned tub.

She forced her gaze away and busied herself retrieving a towel from the cupboard. Water sloshed and splashed behind her as Josh stood and stepped from the tub.

She was about to wrap the towel around her when he reached her.

"What the hell?" His voice sounded just before she felt his hand on her hip. She half turned as he pushed the edge of the towel up and stared at the grapefruit-size bruise marring her pale skin. "What happened?"

"My new tractor. I spent the afternoon trying to tame the yard around this place. It wasn't as easy as I thought it would be. Particularly after paying so much for that blasted tractor."

"How long did you mow?"

"About ten minutes, which ended with me hitting a small tree, flying from the seat and landing on a stump—that's where the bruise came from. Most of the afternoon I spent trying to get the tractor started. Here." She handed him a towel. He was too wet and too aroused and he seemed much too concerned for her peace of mind.

"It's really late." She held the towel protectively under her arms and started for the door. "I really need to get to bed."

"So do I," he murmured. From the hungry look in his eyes, she knew he wasn't talking about his own. A vision of his strong, tanned body against her yellow sheets sent a burst of heat through her, followed by a rush of panic.

"I'll see you tomorrow night," she blurted. "You can see yourself out, can't you?" Without waiting for a reply, she hightailed it from the room and headed down the hall to her bedroom. She felt his gaze on her as she disappeared into the safety of her room and leaned back against the closed door.

She drew a deep, steady breath and listened for his footsteps. It seemed like forever before she heard the thud of boots as he descended the stairs, the slam of her front door, the rev of his truck engine outside. She closed her eyes as the noise faded and she heard only the sound of her own breathing.

Holly retrieved a nightgown from her drawer. Sliding the soft cotton over her head, she pulled back the covers and climbed into bed. The scent of cinnamon and sweet honey clung to her as she crawled beneath the sheets. Her sex ached and she had half a mind to slide her fingers down south and find her own relief. That, or she could use her favorite vibrator sitting in the top drawer of her nightstand.

But the point was to wait. To want. To anticipate. Rose had offered a full, leisurely evening of fun because going slow and taking planned, measured steps heightened the pleasure.

She wasn't going for an orgasm tonight. She was going to close her eyes and go to sleep.

That's what she told herself, but she couldn't manage to doze off. After two long, agonizing hours, she finally gave up and climbed from bed. Her gaze lingered on the nightstand for a few, desperate heartbeats before she reined in her lust and pushed to her feet. Pulling on an oversize T-shirt, she headed downstairs to her kitchen. If she couldn't have a real orgasm, she was going to settle for the next best thing.

She'd eaten half a bowl of cold chocolate batter before the tension in her body eased enough for her to actually breathe again. Breathe, mind you. Sleep was still out of the question. She ate a few more spoonfuls before she calmed down enough to actually turn her attention to the notebook she'd picked up at the Food-o-rama to record her research and make notes for her speech.

Focusing on the process simplified the entire encounter and made her concentrate on the physical put-this-here and touch-this-just-so steps that led to a satisfying experience.

Of course, not complete satisfaction. That would come later. In one week, to be exact. Next Saturday night.

While she'd managed to slice and dice the experience and detach herself from it, the anticipation of what was to come pulled her back to the moment.

To the trembling hands and the aching breasts and the swollen lips, and the fact that Holly wanted Josh McGraw inside of her more than she wanted her next breath.

Understandable. She'd been pretty near celibate for over a year. Once she put her dry spell truly behind her, the fire would die down some.

At least that's what Holly told herself.

7

JOSH TUGGED the chain that hung overhead. The bare
bulb fired to life and pushed back the shadows in the
back area of the main barn. He eyed the tarp that took
up most of the space. A layer of dust coated the beige
covering. Silvery cobwebs filtered from the ceiling,
trembling with the small breeze that filtered through the
open barn door.

Josh reached for the edge of the tarp. His hand trembled, his fingers tight and strained like every other inch
of his body. Christ, he was worked up. More so than
he'd anticipated. Despite the drive home, the air condi-
tioner on high, and a pitcher of ice-cold tea, his body
still burned. He wasn't sure how he'd walked away
from Holly when all he'd wanted to do was push her
up against the bathroom wall and pump fast and furious into her hot little body. But he'd kept his control because he always kept his control. Now was no different.

She was no different.

He ignored the small voice that whispered otherwise
and pulled the tarp. The cover slid to the ground, reveal-
ing the shell of a car beneath.

He forced his thoughts from the image of pale skin

and skimpy black underwear and focused on the 1969 Pontiac GTO. It had been the fastest car to purr down Main Street until the dark night of his mother's death when it had collided with the statue of Romeo McGraw, the town's founder, that had sat in the square in front of city hall. The car had taken out its intended target, and the target had taken out the front end, from the frame to the engine, as well as his father who'd been driving.

The wrecker had hauled it back here all those years ago. Josh's grandfather had parked it in the barn and covered it with the tarp. He'd covered up the truth of his son's death just as easily with a nice, touching story that had painted Walter McGraw a poor, grief-stricken widower who'd driven into the statue and killed himself rather than face the future without his wife who'd died after a difficult miscarriage.

The truth, of course, hadn't been nearly as touching. Guilt had been the driving force behind his father's death. And hatred.

Josh hadn't wanted to look at the damned GTO all those years ago. At the same time, he'd had a deep affection for cars and so he'd eventually pulled back the tarp and started tinkering with it as a teenager. It had been a way to bide his time until his high school graduation and keep his distance from his grandfather. The old man had made it a point to steer clear of the vivid reminder of his only son's stupidity.

Josh had repaired most of the bodywork and had been about to start on the engine when graduation had rolled around. He'd accepted his diploma, said goodbye to his brothers and climbed into his old Chevy and left forever.

Forever had turned out to be a lot shorter than he'd anticipated.

He was back now. Temporarily, of course. Once Mason finished his project and came home, Josh would leave again. He wasn't foolish enough to think it would be forever. As long as his brothers were alive, he would always have ties to Romeo. But it wasn't home. It would never be home.

Never again.

He ran his hand along the primed fender and felt the smooth surface. He'd been young, a novice when it came to bodywork, but he'd still done a halfway decent job. Very few grooves. Only an occasional dip. Of course, he could do a hell of a lot better now. Cars and planes were his specialty. His job. His life.

Yep, he could work wonders with the old GTO if he'd had half a mind. He didn't. He was too busy running the ranch and fulfilling his grandfather's chamber of commerce commitments to have time to tinker with his father's old car.

He glanced inside at the chain-link steering wheel and a memory rushed at him. Of him sitting on his father's lap, his hands gripped around the steering wheel as his dad gunned the engine. A smile tugged at his lips for a long moment before guilt rushed through him and he frowned.

He pulled the tarp back over the frame, killed the light and walked from the barn. It was better to forget the old jalopy. To forget the past.

It was the future that mattered now. Five weeks at the most and his brother would be back. Josh could return to his life then. No more riding fence or branding cattle or branding cattle or birthing calves. Not that he hated those things. They just didn't fill him with the same sense of accomplishment that he felt working on an engine. They didn't offer the same distraction.

He ignored the last thought and walked back into the large ranch house.

"Dangit, Eustace! I was watching that." Great-aunt Lurline's voice carried from the den. "You know I never miss David Letterman."

"They're elk hunting on the Outdoor Channel."

"That's a rerun, you old coot."

"Is not. They hunted exotics last night." Lurline and Eustace were in their eighties and as cranky as all get out. Lurline was Josh's grandfather's sister and she and her husband had been living at the Iron Horse since his grandfather had been diagnosed with prostate cancer. But Josh knew from the holidays and family picnics during his childhood that they'd been arguing a helluva lot longer.

"But Dave's doing his 'Top Ten Reasons to Vote Republican,'" Lurline said.

"You're a Democrat," Eustace pointed out.

"I was a Republican at one time."

"So then you already know the dad-blame reasons and I can watch my elk hunting…."

Josh headed down the opposite hallway, flipped on the TV in his old room and stretched out on the bed. Eustace and Lurline kept going at it and Josh hit the volume button on the remote until their voices faded.

Just as he closed his eyes, his cell phone chirped from the nightstand.

"You have rotten timing," he told his brother when he pressed the on button. "I was actually falling asleep."

"It's not working."

"What's not working?"

"I wore my *I Brake for Big Hooters* T-shirt and showed up with a six-pack of beer instead of a bottle of wine, and it didn't work."

"What happened?"

"Have you ever seen the movie *Species?*"

"Which one?"

"Any of them. All of them. I'm talking major transformation. She went from uptight and proper to loose and damned improper before I could blink much less run the other way."

"What did she do?"

"She asked if she could borrow my shirt sometime and then she drank my beer. The whole six-pack."

"Lots of women like beer."

"Triple B women. She's a *kindergarten* teacher."

"There's no rule that says kindergarten teachers can't drink beer, too."

"She didn't just drink the beer. She guzzled it. And then she tried to kiss me. I mean, I was ready for more baby talk, but the kissing…I couldn't let her kiss me."

"Why not?"

"Because I'd want to kiss her back. You wouldn't believe how hot she looked drinking that beer. Anyhow, if I kissed her back she would think I liked her and, well, I like her, but not enough to trade Junior for Jason. So much for your brilliant idea."

"Maybe she's calling your bluff."

"What do you mean?"

"Maybe she knows you're trying to turn her off, so she's playing along."

"Maybe. She did cough a few times when she first started drinking. And she didn't get specific on *when* she wanted to borrow the shirt. I guess I could try again tomorrow night when she makes chili."

"You agreed to another dinner?"

"I had to. I mean, she looked *really* hot drinking that beer. You know I can't turn down a hot woman any more than I can say no to a crying one. Besides, I've been here for damn near a year and the closest I've come to home cooking is when one of the ranch hands fired up some pork and beans and opened a can of biscuits. Speaking of which, I hope Aunt Lurline makes me a batch of her homemade biscuits when I get home."

"Which will be?"

"I've stepped things up a little for obvious reasons and I think I can squeeze five weeks worth of work into three. Three and a half at the most. I'll talk to you later. Get some rest, bro. You sound exhausted."

Not half as exhausted as he was turned on.

Instead of sleeping, he tossed and turned and dreamed of Holly's sweet hands roaming over his body and her honey-covered nipple in his mouth.

When the sun finally crept over the horizon, Josh felt even more tired than when he'd climbed into bed, and just as unsatisfied. As anxious.

Not that he was going to break the rules of their agreement and rush right over to Holly's house to finish what they'd started. He was going to bide his time until their next encounter.

Or at least until he'd finished his morning chores.

It was half past noon on Monday when Holly finally came up for air after a very hectic morning. She'd found her shipment sitting on her doorstep at 5:00 a.m., and had spent every minute since filling her overdue orders. A task that would have taken all day if not for Sue who'd shown up early for work. The woman had given it her all and they'd finished by eleven o'clock. To show her gratitude, Holly had given the woman an extra half hour for lunch.

Sue had left to run errands in lieu of lunch—she was dieting—and Holly had started on today's orders.

Feeding the desserts into the oven, she set the timer and turned to take a break of her own. She'd just popped the tab on a diet soda when she heard a motor rev to life outside. She walked to the kitchen window and peered past the cherry-print curtains in time to see Josh Mc-Graw shift her brand new John Deere tractor into gear and pick up where she'd left off yesterday afternoon. He wore only jeans, boots, brown work gloves and a cowboy hat. The sun was high and perspiration clung to his shoulders and arms. He toed the clutch with the tip of his worn brown boot and swung the steering wheel to the right. She waited for the possessed piece of machinery to swing the opposite direction and do its own thing as it had done yesterday. Instead, it followed Josh's direction like an obedient puppy and Holly frowned.

Okay, so maybe the frown had more to do with the

half-naked man than the traitorous tractor. While she'd effectively managed to push him to the far edge of her mind and concentrate on her production schedule, the sight of him bare-chested made her heart do a double thump. Damp dark hair pushed from under his hat and clung to his neck. Sweat slid down his sinewy torso. Desire rushed through her full-force and her nipples tingled. Muscles rippled as he gripped the steering wheel and angled the green beast around a patch of bluebonnets contained by a small rock border.

She stared a few more minutes and the tingling spread from her nipples to her thighs. She'd never met a man who inspired such an overwhelming combination of lust and longing. So intense, in fact, that she actually considered joining him in the yard and asking for a ride.

Her imagination sparked and she pictured herself stripping off her shorts and tank top and climbing in front of him. His arms came around, touching her breasts, playing with her nipples before sweeping down between her legs. Fingertips sliding inside of her. Spreading her, working her, driving her completely cra—

"Sorry, I'm late!" Sue's voice rang out, saving Holly from her decadent thoughts. "I had to run a few errands. If I'm going to get Bert Wayne back by being a sex kitten, I figured I should look like one." She deposited several bags on Holly's massive kitchen table. "I went shopping."

Holly eyed the barely there, flaming orange spandex dress that Sue wore. Platform shoes with clear heels and orange glitter toe straps completed the outfit.

"I don't recall seeing a Frederick's of Hollywood the last time I was in town."

"Betty Rinecheck's House of Ho. And it's not exactly in town. Betty's is over in Barton Springs, which is twice the size of Romeo, with two tanning salons and three Piggly Wigglys."

"Definitely an urban metropolis."

"Exactly. Anyhow, I got this…" she motioned to her outfit "…off the spring bargain rack. It was marked down over half off."

"That explains a lot."

"Not that it wasn't one of Betty's hottest outfits. Everyone fell in love with it and a ton of customers tried it on, but they just couldn't pull off this color. I'm a sunrise, which means I look great in vivid colors." She wiggled her fingers. "*And* I got nail polish to match."

"It's bright."

She smiled. "That's the point. Bright says hot, which is the message I'm hoping to send to Bert Wayne." Her gaze went from confident to worried. "I do look hot, don't I? This outfit is guaranteed to make me look hot."

It wasn't the outfit that made her look hot, but rather the lack of outfit. There was very little to it and what *was* there, was so tight that it molded to Sue's body and created an illusion of curves. Lots of them. "You look great."

Her frown eased and she smiled. "Good because I'm putting my win-Bert-back plan into motion next week. I thought I would wear this for spaghetti night at the Elk's Lodge—Bert loves spaghetti." She pulled two slips of paper from her purse and set one on Holly's table. "I picked up two tickets while I was in town. It's the perfect opportunity for you to meet most everyone."

"That many people like spaghetti?"

"It's not just the spaghetti. Warren Parker always shows up with his band—they play over at the Silver Spur every Saturday night. Anyhow, Warren's brother has been an Elk since they first hung up their antlers over at the community center. He has Warren show up to guarantee a big turnout. The folks in this county like to two-step and so the place is usually packed. You should get there early, otherwise you won't get any bread sticks. The folks around here like to eat almost as much as they like to dance." Sue walked past Holly and peered past the cherry-print curtains. "Why is Josh Mc-Graw cutting your grass?"

"I don't know. Maybe it's his way of welcoming me to the neighborhood."

"Josh isn't usually the welcoming sort. I mean, he used to be—nice and all—before his folks died. Then he started to keep to himself. He was still a hell-raiser and every bit the ladies' man, but there was nothing nice about it. He wanted one thing and he made no bones about it. Why, the whole time we were in high school he never once ordered a spirit flower for any of the girls. Even the ones he kept company with. He wouldn't go out of his way like this unless…" Her words trailed off as she seemed to think about what she'd said. "Nah. Not Josh."

"Not Josh what?"

"Nothing."

"Come on."

"Maybe he has a crush and this is his way of getting close to a certain someone."

"And maybe he considers this his land and he doesn't want to see any more butchered because of Beelzebub the tractor."

"Beelzebub looks as docile as a lamb." She stared at Josh a minute more before her smile faded. "Bert Wayne used to mow our grass every Saturday afternoon." She sighed. "I miss those days. The sound of water running and the sputter of that old lawn mower."

"Water running?"

She nodded. "Donna Harper would turn on her water hose and soap up her car and Bert would hightail it out to the shed for the lawn mower. Come to think of it, the only time he would go out to the shed was when Donna was washing her car. Or watering her lawn. He usually power-washed the driveway whenever she saturated her begonias. And he painted the house the summer she planted her vegetable garden."

Holly was about to tell Sue that Bert Wayne sounded like a voyeuristic low-life, but the woman sobbed.

"Who could blame him? It was either stay in the house and see me knit in my sweats or watch Donna prance around in her Daisy Duke's. The poor man. He had no choice." She blinked as if trying to fight back her tears. "I should stop all this yapping. We've got work to do."

Sue started pouring ingredients for the next batch of desserts while Holly went to check on the ones she had in the oven. She tried to ignore the roar of the lawn mower as she went about washing her mixing equipment for the next batch.

A crush?

Right. Like Josh McGraw would have a crush on

her. On any woman, for that matter. He wasn't the type of man to pine away for some woman and drum up excuses to get close to her. He was a straight shooter. A man who went after what he wanted and said exactly what was on his mind.

If you touch me again, I'm going to explode.

His voice stirred in her memory and heat rippled along her nerve endings. She became instantly aware of her hands submerged in the warm water. Bubbles tickled the backs of her fingers and soap slicked her palms and she found herself pulled back in time to their encounter in the bathroom. Her nostrils flared and her fingers flexed as she trailed her sponge over the large beater from her commercial mixer. But she didn't feel cold steel. She felt warm skin and hard muscle and him—

"Knock, knock." The deep male voice slid into her ears and sent a bolt of panic through her. She jumped. The sponge and beater fell from her suddenly limp fingers and plopped into the sink. Water splashed and she whirled to see Josh McGraw standing in her open kitchen doorway.

Where the sight of him several yards away had taken her breath away, having him half-naked and sweaty and barely a few steps away actually stopped her heart. When it did finally start again, it pounded at such a fast, furious rate she was certain it was going to bust out of her chest.

"I didn't mean to startle you. I knocked, but I guess you didn't hear me."

"I was, um, busy." She glanced toward the cooling room where Sue had toted the batch of desserts just pulled from the oven. She glimpsed the woman through the small window as she went about transferring the cakes from the pans to the cooling racks.

Her gaze shifted back to Josh as she realized that she was practically alone with him. What she'd thought of as a large room suddenly seemed much too small, especially when Josh stepped forward and closed the distance between them.

"You're all wet."

"I—I was washing dishes," she blurted, but she knew from the look in his eyes that he wasn't talking about the condition of her shirt. His eyes were too bright, too knowing, too hot. As if he saw the image in her head and was equally turned on.

"What are you doing?"

"Getting a drink."

"That's not what I meant. Why are you here?"

"Maybe I'm being a good neighbor."

"You don't do the neighbor thing."

"Maybe I want you to save your energy for me instead of wasting it on the tractor."

"Maybe."

"Or maybe I'm just here to keep you from making a mess of my property."

"So which one is it?"

"Does it matter?"

It shouldn't, but it did. A realization that sent a burst of panic through her because Holly had already made up her mind to stay indifferent. To keep her distance. Her perspective. Her control.

"There's a pitcher of tea in the fridge. Help yourself."

"Mighty obliged." His Southern drawl rang in her ears as she turned back to the sink and busied herself with the dishes.

She forced herself to concentrate on the dishes rather than his steady footsteps, the sigh of the fridge as he pulled it open, the *clink* of glass as he poured himself a drink, the faint *glug-glug* and his deep, satisfied *ah* when he'd finished.

It wasn't the time or the place, a voice whispered as she gripped the dishes and prayed for him to hurry up.

The screen door finally creaked and the tension eased. She heard the lawn mower start up again. She peered past the curtains in time to see him turn the corner of the house and head for the back pasture area. The sound grew faint and she knew he'd moved farther from the house. Thankfully.

Sue emerged from the cooling room just as Holly rinsed the last beater.

"What next, boss?"

"Paperwork," Holly announced. "I need shipping labels for each order. By then, every thing should be cool enough to box up and ship out."

"If you need me to drive to Cherryville to mail the cakes, I'd be happy to. Or Austin, if you'd rather. There's this great shop down on Sixth Street that I heard about while I was at Betty's."

"More clothes?"

"Sex toys." At Holly's surprised expression, she added, "I figured I could do a little practicing on my own—they custom-make these life-size dolls—until Bert Wayne takes me back. That way I'll be prepared."

"A doll?"

"Not just any old ordinary doll. A *Warm Bodies* doll. It's life-size and anatomically accurate, with skin that warms to the touch. At least that's what Betty said. She said some of her customers have one and swear by him. Say he's better than a boyfriend because he stays hard and he doesn't make any disgusting bodily noises." She smiled. "So if you need me to go, I'd be happy to."

"That would really help me out."

"Then it's settled. You do the labels while I get the boxes ready."

Holly headed into the next room where she plugged her laptop into her printer and started working on the labels.

By four o'clock, Holly's Navigator was filled with the past week's orders. She handed over the keys to Sue, gave her the mailing instructions for each box and retreated inside the house. Josh was still mowing, but he was so far from the house that he was little more than a blur.

Holly put away the last of her equipment and spent the rest of the afternoon going through the second trunk from the attic and doing her best to forget Josh McGraw and the mouthwatering picture he'd made standing in her kitchen doorway, a gleam in his eyes and that sexy-as-hell grin on his face.

She pulled a stack of black-and-white photographs from the trunk and leafed through them. Most were of her mother as a child, her grandmother and the girls who worked the house all those years ago, and a tiny black puppy named T-Bone.

T-Bone's 5th birthday.

She read the scribble on the back of this one picture in particular, before turning it over and studying the young girl holding the excited dog. She marveled that her mother could have loved something so much and never mentioned it. Then again, her mother had rarely talked about her past other than to say that she didn't want to talk about it. Subject closed.

Holly had figured the past was simply too painful for her mother, the memories too hard. But seeing the smiling girl, she couldn't help but wonder if it had been the past that had been so frightening, or leaving that past.

Right. She'd been the daughter of a madam. Of course, she'd run away. She hadn't wanted to join the family business, and so she'd left and made a change. And she'd feared her past catching up to her, dragging her back and making her the same outcast that her mother had been.

At least that's what Holly had initially thought upon learning her grandmother's identity. The explanation fit. At the same time, Holly couldn't quite believe that her grandmother would have forced her lifestyle on any woman. From her records and her personal belongings, Holly got the impression that Red Rose had a big heart. That she cared about people. She didn't seem like the type to force anything on anyone, let alone her young daughter.

The doubts floated through her head as she reached for a stack of old town newspapers that dated back more than half a century—from a fifties issue that depicted the flood that had washed out half the county's pastureland, to the full front page obituary for Tandy Ellen McGraw.

Holly's heart revved when her gaze fell to the small black-and-white photo in the corner of the page. Three teenage boys stood near a flower-laden casket, their heads bowed.

Josh and his brothers.

While triplets, they were fraternal and so they had small, subtle differences. One had hair that seemed lighter than the other two. Another seemed more buff. And then there was Josh. He was a few inches taller than his brothers, his body lean, his shoulders a tad too broad, as if he hadn't quite grown into them yet. He stood between his siblings. At the same time, he seemed set apart. His gaze distant. Pained.

Holly's heart paused and she had the insane urge to trail her fingertips over his face and ease his grief.

She shook away the urge and set the paper aside. It didn't matter what he was feeling because her relationship with him had nothing to do with feeling. It was all about the physical.

She pulled the last stack of photos free and leafed through them before setting them off to the side and pushing to her feet. She plucked at her damp T-shirt and blew out a deep breath.

Downstairs, she poured herself a glass of tea and downed the contents in one long gulp. It did little to cool her overheated body, however. Only one thing could do that.

It's Monday night, remember? Five days from Saturday. Five long days.

Not so long if Josh kept his distance and she kept hers. *Out of sight, out of mind,* she told herself. He'd finished the immediate yard that surrounded the house. The rest was pastureland. There was no reason for her to have any contact with him until their next encounter. Then she could see for herself if the first extreme orgasm had merely been a fluke caused by months of celibacy, or if the chemistry between them really was explosive.

Then, she told herself. And not a minute sooner. No matter how much she wanted to.

8

WHEN HOLLY pictured Duke the delivery guy, she alternated between a maniacal version of Mark Martin racing the back roads of Romeo as if a NASCAR cup waited at the finish line, and one of her second-grade bus driver in Chicago, a retired air force pilot who'd still worn his flight jacket and driven as if half a dozen stealth bombers were trying to sight him in.

Neither image even touched the ancient man standing near the platter of pigs in a blanket at the Monday night Romeo chamber of commerce meeting.

With snow-white hair slicked and combed to the side beneath a blue-and-white Dallas Cowboys cap, a small, stooped body and glasses as thick as the old-fashioned Coke bottles sitting on the refreshment table, he looked like he should be killing time on the back of a tractor rather than a jacked-up Dodge.

"That's Duke Abernathy?" Holly asked Miss Martha who stood next to her and sipped a cup of punch.

"That's him, child."

"No wonder he's slow with deliveries. I can't imagine how he even climbs into his truck, much less peers over the dashboard to drive."

"No, no." Miss Martha shook her head. "That's not Delivery Duke Abernathy. That's old man Duke Abernathy. Duke Junior is over there." She motioned to the man standing next to him. "He does all of the driving and deliveries."

Duke Junior looked to be in his late fifties. He wore a red T-shirt, blue jean overalls and a San Antonio Spurs cap. A can of Skoal peeked over the top of his pocket and his right cheek puffed out like a chipmunk who'd just stashed a few nuts.

"I think I'll introduce myself before the meeting starts."

"I wouldn't do that if I were you. Duke just took up dipping and he's not a very good aim. Last time he talked to Mitchell Winslow, he accidentally nailed him right in the face."

"I'll be careful." She started across the room. "Hi, Mr. Abernathy," she said when she reached the man. "I'm Holly Farraday." She held out her hand.

He eyed her as if she were trying to hand him a nicotine patch. His gray eyebrows drew together. "You're the one who's been leaving complaints on my answering machine."

"That's the voice, all right," said old man Abernathy. "Heard it loud and clear over the Texas A & M post highlights the other day. Why, I missed the winning touchdown 'cause of that."

"I didn't mean to interrupt your game. I was just checking on my orders. I run an Internet-based gourmet dessert business and order my supplies in large quantities. I also use special ingredients that have to be shipped from out of state. None of my orders have arrived on time and I was hoping you could do something about it."

"Like?" Delivery Duke moved his mouth as if shifting the tobacco in his cheek. Before Holly could duck, he lifted a white foam cup to his mouth and spit a stream of brown juice.

She drew a deep breath, tried to calm the sudden pounding of her heart and gave him a hopeful smile. "Move me up on your delivery schedule? Maybe make your more important deliveries first?"

"Important, huh?" He nodded as if she'd just come up with a brilliant idea. "Did you hear that, Dad?" he asked the old man. "Make my important deliveries first. As opposed to my unimportant deliveries."

"Sounds like a plan, Son."

Duke Junior shrugged. "I guess I could tell Mrs. Abercrombie, the old secretary over at the church, that I cain't deliver her diabetic medication on account of you needin' your flour."

"Sure enough," Old Duke agreed.

"And I'm pretty sure Mrs. Daphney over on Fifth Street, who has Parkinson's, could do without those experimental injections from the university for the sake of your sugar. Then there's Mr. Hollingsworth."

"Hollingsworth ain't even sick," the old man offered.

"That's right. Norman, his blue heeler, suffers from a danged awful case of irritable bowel syndrome. He wears these special diapers that come every week from this pet health store up north. But I'm sure ole Norman wouldn't mind losing himself all over the *Reader's Digest* on account of you need vanilla extract."

"Sure, he wouldn't," Old Duke said.

"Then there's Mrs. Mellencamp's weekly care packages from her grandchildren filled with pictures and money and plenty of canned goods 'cause she lives on her Social Security and her loved ones don't want her eatin' dog food. And Jimmy Lee MacIntosh and them there low-carb cookies she special orders online. She's trying to squeeze into her great-great-great-grandma's size-ten wedding dress by the end of the month on account of its a family tradition that ain't been broken in danged near one hundred years. If she ain't got some of those low-carb Oreos when she gets a craving, bam, her wedding day is ruined. But who cares about tradition?"

"Not me," Old Duke said. "'Cept when it comes to the Aggies playing the Longhorns. Why, it's only right that those Aggies whip up on them fancy-pants boys from UT."

"I'm sorry," Holly started. "I didn't realize—"

"You wouldn't," Delivery Duke cut in, "'cause you ain't from around here." He spit another stream of tobacco juice into the cup and turned to the refreshment table. Old Duke followed his lead and Holly found herself staring at their backs.

She turned, her gaze skimming over the room filled with strangers until she found Miss Martha's familiar face. The old woman gave her a little wave before taking a seat at one of the rectangular tables that formed an upside down *U* at the front of the room where the other chamber officers sat.

She recognized a few faces from around town, but she didn't actually know anyone. Her attention shifted to the doorway in time to see Josh McGraw walk through. He smiled at several people before his gaze found hers. Surprise registered, along with a flicker of interest that excited as much as it terrified. It was a re-action she'd felt many times in her life when she'd been in a new situation, standing on the outside and desper-ately wanting *in*.

At the same time, it was much more intense than any-thing she'd ever felt. And that was much more frighten-ing because there was so much more at stake.

Her future.

Her heart.

She ignored the last thought and concentrated on taking a deep, measured breath.

Get out of here, a voice whispered. *Just start walk-ing and don't look back. You don't belong.*

Maybe not. But she was going to try.

Holly forced her gaze from Josh, stepped toward the first row of chairs and took a seat right in the middle.

JOSH HAD SPENT the entire afternoon on the back of a trac-tor, with the full intent of working himself past the point of exhaustion. Past the point of wanting anything—Holly included—beyond a soft bed and some blessed quiet.

But as he sat two rows behind her at the chamber of commerce meeting, need rose, sharp and demanding, in-side of him.

He crossed his arms and tried to stare past her, to con-centrate on chamber president Dr. Stewart Connally, the town pediatrician, who stood behind the podium and led the meeting. But Josh couldn't seem to help

himself. Holly was a damned sight better to look at than
old Stewart. She wore a trendy pink T-shirt that hugged
her full breasts, the slogan *Girls Rock* in silver glitter,
and snug Levi's that made him wonder how she'd managed to wiggle into them, and how he'd like to peel them
right off. She'd pulled her long hair back into a ponytail and slicked her lips with a soft pink gloss. The heels
on her black leather cowboy boots were a little too high
to be practical, but the toes had scuffed up nice thanks
to her gravel driveway. Overall, she looked comfortable
and relaxed and down-home, as if she really and truly
belonged in Romeo.

To make matters worse, she volunteered for three
different committees, and offered up two dozen desserts for the upcoming bake sale benefiting the local library.

And damned if he didn't want her in spite of it all.

Because of it.

She had balls. Small towns, Romeo included, tended
to have a country club mind-set. If you weren't a "member," you weren't welcome, period. There wasn't a vis-
itor's bureau in the heart of downtown. It was the sort
of place where everyone knew everyone, and until folks
really got to know you—provided they even bothered—
they were suspicious and downright cold.

The meeting was a prime example. Holly sat by herself. Sure, Jim Riley sat on one side and Delilah Max-
well sat on the other because they'd come in late and all
the other seats had been taken, but neither spoke to her.
Hell, they didn't even spare her a smile.

Holly didn't seem the least bit affected. She sat up

straight and proud and looked as comfortable as if this were her hundredth meeting rather than her first.

His chest tightened and warmth seeped through him. A feeling that had nothing to do with lust and everything to do with admiration. He'd had his own home pulled out from under him and he knew what it was like to feel like an outsider.

But at least he'd had his brothers. After her mother had died, she'd been on her own.

She was still on her own.

"…anyone willing to stay after tonight's meeting to help sort and box the school clothes for the needy families, please raise your hand."

Her long, willowy fingers slid into the air for the countless time that night.

"I have one volunteer. Any others? It's for a good cause."

Before Josh could stop himself, he raised his own hand.

"There we have it, folks. A dynamic duo."

Holly turned and their gazes met. Her full lips formed a surprised *You?* If there hadn't been two rows separating them, he would have been hard-pressed not to kiss her. As it was, he was just hard.

But the attraction between them went deeper than the heat prickling his skin and the hunger gnawing at his gut. Even more than wanting her, he connected with her. He understood the desperation that drove her. And the loneliness. He'd felt them both all those years ago after his parents had died.

Hell, he still felt them every once in a while. In the dead of night when sleep refused to come and the memories crept up on him. But the feelings quickly faded into the regret that ate away at him and refused him any peace.

For now.

But he was changing that. He was putting the Iron Horse back together and absolving himself.

"I really don't think this is a good idea," she told him when the meeting adjourned and he met her in the far corner of the room where the clothing donations had been stacked.

He winked. "And here I thought you were the charitable sort."

"I don't mean this." She motioned around her at the donations. "I mean you and me."

He arched an eyebrow. "Afraid you won't be able to keep your hands off me?"

"Hardly. The whole point—" she started to say, but her words were drowned in the loud greeting that carried from across the room.

"Holly!"

They both turned to see Lolly Langtree and Jennifer Something-or-other—Josh wasn't sure of her last name because she'd been married four times and was obviously anxious for number five if she kept company with the president of the Juliets. Both women smiled and waved.

"So nice to see you," Lolly called out.

Holly's full lips curved into a dazzling smile that slid between his ribs and stalled the breath in his lungs. "Nice to see you, too," she called out.

"The girls and I are counting down the days to the luncheon!"

Holly's smile faltered just a little. "Um, me, too."

Worry flickered in her gaze and Josh had the sudden urge to pull her close and tell her everything was going to be all right.

Instead, he murmured, "Me, three," when she turned back to him.

She eyed him. "You won't be at the luncheon."

"No, but I get to be at the research sessions which are a helluva lot more fun than a bunch of desperate women sipping tea and nibbling cookies."

He could have sworn her lips hinted at a grin, but then her expression grew serious. "You really don't have to stay and help. I can sort this stuff myself."

"I volunteered."

"So did I, but only because I want to get to know the members of the community."

"I'm a member."

"A temporary one."

"Meaning it's pointless to get to know me."

"I think I know you well enough."

"You'll know me a lot better before it's all said and done, cupcake." His voice was deep and husky as he leaned just a little too close, his hand brushing hers as he reached for a nearby box.

Hunger flared in her gaze. But then she stiffened and her expression became guarded. "I really think we should get to work." She turned away and put some distance between them as she retrieved a large stack of boys' blue jeans.

The minutes ticked by as Josh put together the empty boxes and taped up the bottoms while Holly sorted the clothes.

"So you're a pilot?" Her soft voice eventually broke the silence.

"I run a charter service out of Phoenix, Arizona. I've got an apartment there, but I don't get home much. I fly a lot."

"I was in Phoenix once. My mother and I lived there for about four months before we moved to Kansas City."

"I thought you grew up in Chicago?"

"I grew up everywhere. Phoenix. Kansas City. Denver. Houston. New Orleans. Chicago." Her hands faltered on a pair of jeans and they slipped from her hands. "We were living in Chicago when she died."

"How old were you?"

"Eight."

"What about your dad?"

"I never knew him, and my mom really didn't, either. She was young and vulnerable and lonely, and he was little more than a one-night stand. She contacted him after the fact and told him about the pregnancy and he urged her to have an abortion. She refused and decided to raise me alone." Her lips trembled and he had the sudden urge to slide an arm around her, pull her close and simply hold her. And talk to her.

Christ, he was friggin' crazy. Most of his time with the opposite sex had been spent between the sheets or in the cockpit of his airplane or on top of his kitchen table—anywhere the carnal urge might strike. He'd never really talked to a woman before. Sure, he'd had a few try to talk to him, but he'd always been too busy to take the time.

Hell, he'd never *wanted* to take the time.

Until now.

"Denver's one of my favorite cities," he heard himself say. "There's nothing more beautiful than cruising over snow-capped mountains."

She shrugged. "It *was* pretty, but I liked Houston the best. That's why I moved there to start my business." Her gaze twinkled. "I never would have figured you for a snow bunny."

"I like the way it looks from the cockpit of a plane, but I'd trade freezing my nuts off for a Texas summer any day." His grin faded as he eyed her. "I like it hot."

How hot?

The question was there in her gaze. In the way her chest hitched and her nipples pebbled beneath the pink T-shirt. In the sudden color that flushed her cheeks and the way her tongue darted out to slick the plump fullness of her bottom lip.

"The old folks around here call it Texas Fever. They say when it reaches a certain temperature outside, it causes a light-headedness that can be addictive."

"Do you believe that?"

He shrugged. "I know I like it hot enough that it gets hard to breathe. So hot you can't really think anymore." He pinned her with a gaze and his voice grew husky. "So hot the only thing you can do is feel."

Sweaty skin and damp sheets and one body driving into the next.

She turned, as if his answer was more than she'd bargained for, and busied herself for several tense moments.

"So how long have you been flying?" she finally asked, as if she needed to do something with her mouth.

He knew the feeling. He wanted to do something with his own mouth, but all of the possibilities were sure to get him arrested. It was a public meeting hall, after all, and a few of the commerce members lingered here and there, finishing off the refreshments and catching up on the latest gossip.

He licked his lips, ignoring the urge to pull her close and take a long, delicious taste of her and focused on the memories stirring inside of him. "I got my pilot's license when I was nineteen."

"Did you always want to be a pilot?"

"I didn't plan it. I used to have a thing for cars back in high school. It was the one thing me and my dad did together before he died. He had a special thing he did with each of us individually so that we didn't have to share everything in our lives. That's what usually happens with most multiples. They wind up sharing everything. But not us. Not with my dad."

"Sounds like he was a good man."

"When it came to being a dad. He wasn't much of a husband, but then my parents weren't exactly a love match." He wasn't sure why he'd told her that. The words just came out and he hadn't tried to stop them. "My dad was set to inherit the biggest ranch in the Hill Country and my mom was the only child of the owner of the second biggest spread. It only made sense that they join forces and make the Iron Horse that much bigger."

"Especially since your grandfather had given some of it away to his mistress."

"I'm sure that was the thinking at the time."

"So your father didn't love your mother?"

"Are you kidding?" He shrugged. "I don't think he ever believed in the concept. I know she didn't."

"How do you know that?"

"She told me so the night she died." *Enough,* a voice whispered. The same voice that told him to walk away whenever any woman tried to get into his head, in addition to his bed.

But Holly didn't want to get close to him. She wanted sex.

"She'd had a hard time getting pregnant with me and my brothers," he heard himself say. "We were the result of several years of fertility treatments. She didn't think she could ever conceive again, but she did. Sixteen years later."

"She had another baby?"

He shook his head. "She started bleeding one evening and had to be rushed to the hospital over in Cherrywood. She found out she was pregnant and having a miscarriage all in the same night. My father should have been there with her, but he wasn't." His gaze met Holly's. "He was out with another woman."

"He had a girlfriend while he was married to your mother?"

"He had a lot of girlfriends. I didn't know who he was with, but I knew what he was doing. She knew it, too, but she asked me anyway."

"What did you tell her?"

"That he was playing poker at the Elk's Lodge. That's when she told me that it didn't matter anyway. She'd never loved him and he'd never loved her and their marriage had been one of convenience." He wiped a hand over his eyes, as if he could blot out the image of his mother staring back at him from the hospital bed, her eyes knowing. Filled with disappointment. "She didn't want me to, but I went looking for him anyway. By the time I found him and we got back to the hospital, it was too late." At her questioning look, he added, "They did a D&C, but something went wrong and her uterus ruptured. She bled to death before anyone realized what was happening. When my dad heard the news, he felt so guilty that he took off like a bat out of hell and wrapped his GTO around a telephone pole. Just like that, they were both gone and it was just me, my brothers and my grandfather."

"I'm so sorry."

"It all happened really fast. At the same time, it was the longest night of my life."

"I know the feeling."

"How's that?"

"I was only eight when my mom was killed in a car accident. But it wasn't instantaneous. She lingered in the hospital for twenty-six hours. I tried to see her, but they wouldn't let me. I had to sit in the waiting room with one of our neighbors." She shook her head and her eyes took on a pained light. "I knew she was hurt, but I didn't think she was going to die." She blinked at the sudden brightness that filled her eyes. "I just wish I had been able to see her one last time." She shook her head. "So what was your special thing with your dad?"

"He and I worked on cars. With my middle brother, Mason, he roped calves and helped him with his rodeoing. With my youngest brother, Rance, he played touch football."

"Rance? Why does that name sound familiar?"

"He played pro ball for the Dallas Cowboys after college. He took them to several play-offs before he injured his knee."

"I guess we're all drawn to the familiar." She set a stack of neatly folded blue jeans in a box and taped it up. "Like me and my baking."

"Your mother used to bake?"

She nodded. "One of the many jobs my mother had was at a bakery in Houston. They didn't pay very well, but they let her bring home the leftovers. Cookies. Cupcakes. Pies. I was only little, but I remember waiting up every night for her and that white bakery bag. When I opened it, there was always this sweetness that filled the air. When she died, one of the things I missed most was that smell."

"So you bake because the smell reminds you of her."

"Actually, I bake to make money, which is why I specialize in aphrodisiac desserts."

"Because sex sells?"

She nodded. "But I first started back in college because it helped me feel a little less lonely. That's probably why you're so into planes." At his puzzled glance, she added, "Because they remind you of the cars, which remind you of your dad."

"A Cessna is a far cry from a Corvette."

"Obviously, but under the hood they probably have a few similar parts."

He shook his head as if to dismiss the notion, but it stayed with him long after they'd finished boxing up the donated clothes and he watched her climb into her Navigator.

Because deep down Josh feared she was right.

HOLLY WAS *this close* to having a major meltdown.

Both physically—from the lust blazing inside of her—as well as mentally—small-town living could be a *major* bitch.

She stood on her front porch early Friday morning and stared at the taillights of Duke's pickup as it disappeared up the road. With the special ingredients, namely wild green oats and saw palmetto berries, she'd ordered online Wednesday afternoon. She had no doubt that the herb company had shipped everything as requested. For over two years, her shipments had come from Herb Express like clockwork.

Until she'd moved to Romeo.

Okay, a voice whispered. *So you didn't get it yesterday and you're not getting it first thing this morning? That doesn't mean Duke won't stop by later in the day. He knows who you are now and you're obviously making an effort to get to know him. He's just busy delivering a heart or an aesthetic limb or some other must-have, and he'll get to you soon.*

She clung to the hope and turned to walk back into the house. She had half a mind to head upstairs and crawl back into bed. Exhaustion tugged at every muscle. Her eyes felt gritty and sandy.

At the same time, her heart pumped faster than usual and expectancy fluttered in the pit of her stomach. There was no way she could fall back to sleep.

As if she'd slept in the first place.

Rather, she'd spent the night tossing and turning and fantasizing about Josh McGraw and the next recipe.

About tonight.

She forced aside the thought as she walked into her kitchen. Right now, she had work to do. The last thing she needed was to think about Josh spread out on the sofa in room number four. Wearing nothing but several well-placed pineapple rings and a smile. Her tummy tingled and her hands trembled.

So much for not thinking about him.

She reached her daily production grid and managed to sort ingredients. She'd just folded in some freshly ground coriander for a batch of Venus Vanilla Mousse when she heard the rattle of Sue's orange Honda.

Not too shabby for a woman on the edge.

"Mornin'." Sue wobbled through the kitchen door on two-inch red stilettos with straps that wound up her calves. A red spandex tube dress clung to her thin frame, pushing and pulling with each step. Crimson lipstick and black-rimmed eyes completed today's sex kitten ensemble. She hooked her purse near the door, tugged at the bodice of her dress and reached for her apron.

Her gaze was expectant when she turned back to Holly. "Did Duke make it by here?"

"He sure did." Sue smiled, but the expression died when Holly added, "He drove right in front of me without so much as tapping the brakes."

She shook her head. "I'm sure he'll make it by later."

Holly poured the contents of the mixing bowl into a

baking pan and barely resisted the urge to grab a spoon and scrape the bottom.

She wasn't upset or uptight. Upset or uptight meant vanilla and she was determined to have more of a calm, chocolate mint sort of day.

"We'll keep our fingers crossed," Sue added.

"I think it's going to take more than that." Holly fed the pan into the oven and set the timer.

"Like what?"

"How are you at human sacrifice?"

"If the human in question is a bleached blonde with big boobs and Daisy Duke shorts, I'm good to go."

Holly grinned, but it did little to ease her overall worry. While she'd been stockpiling extra supplies with daily trips to the Food-o-rama, she'd accumulated just enough basic ingredients to get her through today which marked a whopping three days since Duke's first and last delivery. The manager, a sour-faced Mr. Morton, had confronted her yesterday in front of the vanilla extract and informed her that the store had a quantity limit on all items—namely all of the items in her basket. She remembered the conversation quite clearly.

"We are a small establishment, Ms. Farraday, and we have other customers besides you. Regular customers."

"I understand that, but I'm not getting timely deliveries and—"

"Our own deliveries only come once a week and Ida Sinclair has already filed a formal complaint because she came in to buy a bottle of vanilla extract to make pinwheel cookies for the Senior Ladies' Social and we were out." He pinned her with a stare. *"Because of*

you." His mouth drew into a razor-sharp line. "The senior ladies need their cookies, Ms. Farraday. When they don't get their cookies, they get cranky. When they get cranky, they get mean. When they get mean, they make life a living hell for their middle-aged sons who are forced to live at home because of ridiculous alimony payments to fund an ex-wife's liposuction habit."

"I don't mean to inconvenience anyone. I'm just trying to make do until my deliveries get straightened out."

He gave her a tight smile. "Let's both be realistic. That could take a while. In the meantime, I have steady customers—customers who've been patronizing this store for years—who depend on the Food-o-rama. We're the only grocery for sixty-eight-point-four miles."

"Sixty-eight-point-eight."

Surprise flickered in his gaze and she knew she'd impressed him. Not that he would admit it, she realized when he frowned again and told her, "I can't very well disappoint and upset my steady, reliable customers simply because you're in a fix."

Meaning she wasn't one of the steady, reliable customers. She was an outsider. And she was SOL—shit out of luck.

It wasn't a total disaster, mind you, just an aggravation that made living in Romeo that much more difficult. She could pick up her standard baking supplies at any number of the grocery stores when she drove into Cherryville to send out her shipments. The special ingredients that made her desserts a hot commodity would be harder to come by. She doubted the Cherryville Piggly Wiggly carried yohimbe bark or damiana leaves.

Only a good herbalist stocked those, and the closest Herbs & Other Good Stuff sat over one hundred miles away in Austin.

That meant a two-hour drive each way. Add shopping time to that and she would waste at least six hours. Which meant she would have to make up the lost kitchen time on Sunday.

She'd worked Sundays before. Heck, she'd worked every Sunday for the past five years. But that was then and this was supposed to be now—the start of a new life in a new place with new priorities. She was building a home for herself and planting roots and a garden. She also had her grandmother's things to finish packing away, and desserts to bake for the chamber's upcoming bake sale, and she still had to figure out the infamous house special. She hadn't found anything in her grandmother's records, but the house special was legend in Romeo.

An image rushed at her of a very hard, very naked Josh spread out on her bed, his hands and feet tied to the bedposts. He wore a blindfold and an expression of pure ecstasy as she trailed the tip of a leather whip over his hard six-pack.

Then again, she might be the one tied to the bedposts while a very hard, very naked Josh trailed the tip of a leather whip from her breasts down to her—

Her nipples tingled and she clenched her thighs together.

She'd never been into bondage, be it as the dominator or the dominatee, but if the house special called for it, she would certainly be willing to try in the interest of research.

If.

She didn't know. She hoped that the answer lay somewhere in the house, in one of her grandmother's trunks or one of the specialty rooms, and she meant to find it before their last encounter.

In the meantime, she did her best to lose herself in her work and forget that tonight was *the* night.

She'd thought that scheduling their time together would help her keep her perspective about the whole thing and kill the anticipation. But it only heightened the sensation. By the time the afternoon rolled around and she finally climbed into her Navigator to head into town for the necessary ingredients for recipe five—Rose's wildly popular Pineapple Upside Down Cake—her hands actually trembled and her heart pounded.

Then again, maybe it wasn't sexual anticipation, she decided when she stopped off at the small house that sat on the edge of town. Maybe her system was out of whack because of sheer stupidity.

She'd never been one to go back for a second helping of humiliation. In the past, she hadn't really cared if people had liked her. In fact, she'd wanted them not to like her. It made leaving that much easier.

Not this time.

She retrieved a boxed dessert from her backseat and started up the front walk. Dogs barked and a sports announcer's voice carried through the screen door as she approached.

"…at the first down and—holy moly, it's a touchdown!"

She knocked and pasted on her best smile when Old Duke Abernathy pushed open the screen door.

"What's this?" he asked when she handed him the box.

"Just a little something for your son to say I'm sorry for the other day at the commerce meeting. I didn't mean to sound pushy."

"Sorry, huh?" He lifted the lid and eyed the contents. "You ought to be, seein' as how you badgered him and all, but I'm afraid my boy cain't do dairy. It messes him up somethin' awful. Everybody knows that." He peered at her over his thick bifocals. "Where you from again?"

"I've been living in Houston for the past five years."

He snorted. "Never did like those Astros much. I've always been a Texas Rangers fan, myself. Me and my boy." He paused to glance behind him at the television and let loose a loud, crackling, "Interception, dammit. *Interception!*"

"I'll let you get back to the game. Sorry about the dairy situation. I'll just take this back—"

"Not so fast. Seein' as how you went to all the trouble to bring this out here, the least I can do is put it to good use."

"Of course." She smiled. "I hope you enjoy it."

"Not me. Dairy messes me up somethin' awful, too. But Sassy and Frassy out back are sure to love it."

"Sassy and Frassy?"

He grinned. "My hogs."

9

THE SUN WAS just setting when Josh arrived at the Farraday Inn and found the recipe taped to Holly's front door. No urgent kisses in the doorway. No frantic fumbling in the foyer. No heat burning them both up from the inside out. No Holly. Nothing but an index card with specific instructions.

1. Go upstairs to dining room five.

2. Remove all clothing.

He pushed open the door, mounted the stairs for the second floor and walked down the hall to the designated room.

A brocade rug covered most of the hardwood floor. Throw pillows filled every nook and cranny. Old-fashioned hurricane wall sconces hung from each of the four walls. The flames flickered, casting shadows on the gold-and-red wallpaper. A large red leather settee sat in the center of the room. A cherrywood sideboard held a large gold serving tray covered with chunks of pineapple and maraschino cherries. Rich brown sugar glaze filled a matching gold gravy boat. The ripe scent of fruit filled the air and flared his nostrils.

Sinking down on the red leather, he tugged off his boots and socks, his ears alert for the sound of her footsteps.

Nothing. Just the thunder of his own heart and a voice that told him he didn't like this. Not one little bit.

He pushed to his feet, gripped the hem of his T-shirt and pulled it up and over his head. Soft, worn cotton slithered over his skin and heightened the anticipation coiling in his stomach. His fingers went to the waistband of his jeans and he slid the button free. He grabbed the tab of his zipper only to hesitate. While he fully intended to comply with her instructions, he wasn't doing it yet.

Not without her.

"You're not naked." Her soft, accusing voice drew him around. He turned to find her standing in the doorway. She wore a short black satin robe. Thigh-high black stockings hugged her shapely legs. Tiny red bows decorated the top of each stocking and drew his attention to the pale slice of thigh visible between the stocking and the robe. The urge to touch the smooth expanse of bare skin nearly doubled him over.

"Nice outfit."

"Thanks, but nice isn't exactly the look I'm going for. I was trying for something a little more provocative."

She spoke as boldly as she had in the bathroom during the appeteasers, her gaze as hot and bright and needy. He found himself wondering if he'd just imagined the push-pull of emotion in her expression at the chamber of commerce meeting. As if she'd been fighting her attraction to him.

She didn't seem the least bit conflicted now.

Strictly business.

Her words echoed in his head and he stiffened, suddenly as annoyed as he was turned on.

But then she stepped forward and touched him, and everything faded in the soft press of her fingertips against his bare stomach.

"Let me help you with those." She gripped his zipper and his breath caught. Metal hissed and the zipper eased and desire knotted in his gut.

Josh had always been the one to take the lead and do the undressing. The looking was the best part, or so he'd always thought. Until that moment.

Holly slipped her satiny fingers inside the elastic of his BVDs and tugged them down. Her fingertips grazed his skin and her gaze seared him, and he burned even hotter than if he'd been the one peeling the robe from her soft, pale body.

She worked the clothing down his hips until his erection bobbed free. She stopped then, her attention fixed on his throbbing cock and a strange mix of emotion swirled inside him. Half of him wanted to haul her into his arms and kiss her tenderly while the other half wanted to bend her over and drive into her like a man possessed.

He did neither. It was her recipe and she was the one doing the cooking.

For now.

She licked her lips and he could have sworn he felt the slick glide of her tongue on his throbbing cock. His breath hitched and his heart hammered and... *Shit*, he was hard.

She tugged his jeans and underwear down to his ankles and he stepped free. Then she leaned back on her haunches and let her gaze take a slow trek up the length of his body. "I think we're just about ready."

"I've been ready, cupcake."

She smiled. "No cupcake tonight. We're having upside-down cake." She motioned him to the settee as she pushed to her feet and retrieved the large serving tray.

He stretched out and watched the gentle sway of her ass beneath the shiny black robe as she retrieved the large serving tray. She returned to the settee and sat in the spot where he'd left room for her. Placing the tray on the floor, she retrieved a chunk of pineapple. Before she could place it on his navel, he took her hand and guided her fingers into his mouth.

The sweet taste exploded on his tongue and he groaned.

Or maybe it was the way she retrieved a piece of pineapple and lifted it to her own mouth that made him groan. Her teeth sank into the fruit and juice slicked her lips and his stomach hollowed out.

Either way, the sound echoed, followed by the sharp intake of his breath when she reached for the brown sugar syrup and dribbled it into his navel and lower, until she'd drenched his cock. The warm stickiness trickled down his balls and between his legs, and raw heat erupted inside of him.

She leaned forward then and drew him into her mouth. She licked and suckled and devoured every drop of sauce, and it was all Josh could do not to explode right then and there.

But he wanted to taste her the way she was tasting him and feel her vibrate against his lips. He wanted them in sync.

As if Holly read his thoughts, she leaned away from

him and reached for her robe. The slinky material parted and slid from her shoulders until she wore nothing but the thigh-high stockings.

He reached out and touched her ripe nipple and relished the gasp that parted her lips. Before he could sit up and pull her to him, she pulled back and dipped her fingers into the brown sugar sauce.

With her gaze locked with his, she circled her belly button before leaving a golden trail as she moved lower, spreading the sauce down her abdomen to her sex. She dipped her fingers between her lips and spread the sauce between her legs. Her breath caught and her chest hitched and he watched as she slipped a finger inside.

It was the most erotic thing Josh had ever seen and hunger gripped him hard and fast, and he reached for her.

He caught her waist and urged her around until her luscious bottom faced him. He gripped her thigh and lifted it over his body, pulling her up and over him until her thighs rested on either side of his head and the heart of her lingered near his mouth.

At his first long, slow lick, Josh felt Holly shudder. The next lick was even slower, longer. Her arms and legs trembled. She seemed paralyzed for the next few moments as he savored her. But when he pressed his tongue into her soft folds and drew her clit into his mouth, a moan burst from her lips.

She dipped her head then and drew him into her mouth. The more he sucked and licked, the longer and harder she loved him with her mouth until he felt her body stiffen and he knew she was close.

He gripped her thighs and held her tight as he devoured her, until her essence exploded on his tongue. He followed her over the edge and she stayed with him until the very end, her sweet mouth loving him more thoroughly than any in his past.

Or his future.

Before Josh could think on the notion, Holly eased away from him and reached for her robe.

"You know the way out," she told him before she disappeared and he was left feeling as if he'd just been stood up.

She didn't stand you up, guy. She got you up, and then she let you down. Big difference.

But as Josh pulled on his clothes, he didn't feel any more satisfied than he had when he'd walked into the Farraday Inn. For the first time, he found himself doubting all the rumors he'd grown up hearing about the Farraday Inn.

"Satisfaction guaranteed? My ass."

HOLLY DREW a deep breath and finished writing the last of her notes on tonight's encounter.

Her mouth watered for a bite of chocolate batter as she closed her spiral notebook and set it on her shelf next to her recipe books. Josh had left over a half hour ago and her body still hummed. Her heart hammered. Her blood rushed. Her thighs tingled. *Ugh.*

It was not supposed to be this way.

Sure, she could understand why she'd had a whopper of an orgasm their first night together. She'd been coming off a long dry spell and he'd been really hot and she'd been lonely and…well, he'd been *really* hot.

But every dessert chef worth her whipped cream knew that the second bite was never quite as good as the first.

Then again, tonight *had* been different. It wasn't as if he'd actually been inside of her, and she'd exploded like a blender with the top off. Unlike their first time, they hadn't actually had *sex*. Rather, they'd pushed the boundaries and livened up the foreplay in a way that had been fresh and exciting and extremely tasty. Anyone with a pulse and some taste buds would have been hard-pressed not to have a cataclysmic orgasm.

Tomorrow night wouldn't be nearly as mind-blowing. Recipe six was next on the list, and just reading it made Holly wince. She doubted even a humdrum orgasm would come of it. Even so, she was going to work herself up and set off a few Roman candles prior to his arrival so that she would be completely relaxed and sated and not the least bit horny. Then if she saw fireworks, she would know that her attraction to Josh went deeper than anything she'd ever felt before.

Not that it mattered, mind you.

She still wasn't going to fall for him. He was temporary and she wasn't.

Never again.

THERE WAS A naked man sitting in her kitchen.

Holly blinked against the bright morning sunlight spilling through the kitchen curtains and focused on the large, muscular body seated at her kitchen table, his back to her.

Her gaze finally focused and she drank in the tanned

skin and round buttocks and long legs curled around the edge of the chair and...

Ohmigod! There was a *naked* man sitting in her kitchen.

Correction—a naked *stranger*.

She couldn't see his face, but she could see enough to know that he wasn't anyone she knew, especially Josh. Blond hair curled down around his neck. His shoulders weren't quite as broad, his arms not nearly as muscular. Even so, she had no doubt he could slide his hands around her neck and squeeze the life out of her if she didn't do something right now.

Run!

She wanted to, but her keys to both the van and her Navigator sat on the opposite cabinet, which meant she would be running for several miles before she reached the nearest neighbor. The chances of him tackling her before she could get help were overwhelming, which meant she would have to fight him off.

Her mind raced and she reached for the large mixing spoon that sat on a nearby cabinet. A *spoon?* What was she going to do? Stir him to death?

Her fingers closed just shy of the spoon and she grabbed the small pastry torch she used to brown the coconut for her Venus Vanilla Mousse. It was heavy enough to clock him if she could get in a good swing before he happened to see—

"They sent the wrong man."

Holly whirled at the sound of Sue's voice and the torch fell from her suddenly limp fingers. Metal crashed against the hardwood floor. Her heart rammed into her rib cage and she whirled back to see him bolt to his feet and—

He didn't so much as budge.

"He was waiting on the doorstep along with your stuff." Sue walked around her toward the table. She wore her work apron, a reminder that Holly had slept right through her alarm. And the roar of Duke's truck and the screech of his brakes.

"He stopped?" Holly pushed open the screen door to see the stack of boxes that sat on her front porch. "He did. He actually stopped." She smiled as she eyed the familiar label from her herb company. "I may end up liking that man, after all."

"That makes one of us. I don't understand it. I filled out the order form and gave specific instructions. I can't use a blonde. Bert has brown hair. It would feel too much like cheating and the whole point is to pretend like he's Bert, so that when it really is him, I'll be ready to go."

Holly let the screen door close and turned back to Sue. "What are you talking about?"

"The *Warm Bodies* company sent me the wrong doll."

Her gaze swiveled to the naked stranger. "You mean that's a *doll?*"

"A very expensive doll. I used my entire savings to pay for Billy the Buckaroo. He comes with a cowboy hat and spurs and looks the most like Bert." She shook her head. "This is Paul the Preppie." She motioned to the paperwork that sat on the table along with a black silk tie and a pair of designer socks. "The company got my order mixed with someone else's, but they said they'll send me the correct one just as soon as I send this back."

A *doll*.

The truth echoed in Holly's head and calmed her pounding heart as she approached the table and rounded the figure sitting in the chair.

Forget the cheesy blow-up sex toys she'd seen in the movies. Despite the stiffness of his body, this doll looked like a bona fide, life-size man, complete with a sprinkle of golden hair on his chest and a limp member resting on top of two rather large testicles. Of course, the member was wrapped in plastic, tape covered his eyes and he had foam stuffed into his mouth. But otherwise, the likeness was remarkable.

Sue's gaze twinkled. "If you stroke it, it gets bigger."

Holly grinned. "No way."

"Way. It has this built-in pump that responds to heat." At Holly's disbelieving look, she added, "His skin is made from a special silicone mixture that warms to the touch just like the real thing. Try it." Sue motioned to the bare skin of his shoulder and Holly reached out.

"It's soft, supple and—" her gaze collided with Sue's "—it *is* warm. And getting warmer."

"I told you. He's made from the same stuff they use on the space shuttle and his hair is made from this special synthetic that feels as soft as silk. He's also waterproof so you can take him into the shower or a hot tub, and he's even got a tongue and a mouth that moves when you press this button at the back of his neck."

"Now that sounds kind of creepy."

"I guess it does, doesn't it?" Sue eyed the doll. "Okay, kissing is out—it's too intimate—but he's good for lots of other things." Her eyes twinkled. "His thingamajig has three different speeds and is the ultimate vibrator. I can definitely use him to practice my lap dancing." Her brows drew together. "Once I exchange him, that is."

"You're taking lap dancing lessons?"

"It's a home video course I ordered from this magazine. It even comes with this numbered diagram—sort of like a *Twister* board—that you place on your man's lap to help you touch all the right parts." She grabbed the plastic bag and slid it over Paul's head. She hefted him into her arms and placed him in a large box that sat off to the side of the kitchen, his legs hanging over the side. "I'll bend him back up and ship him back on Monday when we send out our orders."

"Speaking of orders, we'd better get to work." Holly reached for her own apron and started unpacking and sorting supplies.

She spent the rest of the day baking her back orders while Sue boxed the desserts and slid them into the freezer to be shipped on Monday. They finished around five in the afternoon. Sue left to pick up a pizza and spend Saturday evening watching her *Sex and the City* DVD collection while Holly headed upstairs to the sixth dining room to prepare for tonight's recipe.

The room had been decorated in various shades of blue, from the sheer curtains that covered the windows to the bedspread draping the full-size bed. The color said calm. Easy. Relaxed.

She would have to be if she intended to masturbate in front of Josh McGraw.

She'd never actually gone solo in front of any man

before and doubt tied knots into her stomach. At the same time, a thrill of excitement rippled up her spine as she arranged the massage oils and lubricants she'd picked up while sending out her last shipment. She'd also picked up a new toy. She opened the drawer and pulled out a bright pink rectangular box.

The purpose of tonight's recipe—Hot-from-the-oven, Hand-picked Cherry Pie—was to give Josh a show that would have him getting off while watching her, and so Holly wanted to be completely prepared. The lady at the adult goody shop had said this was the latest and greatest vibrator on the market. Much better than the tried-and-true version Holly kept in her own nightstand drawer, and more impersonal. There was just something about using her own in front of him that seemed, somehow, so…*intimate*.

This wasn't about intimacy. It was about sex. And so she was getting jiggy with *The Rabbit*.

Pulling the contraption from the box, Holly tested the batteries and set it on the nightstand before heading back downstairs. Just as she'd done the night before, she taped an index card with instructions for tonight's recipe to the kitchen door for Josh. The less contact she had with him outside of the dining room, the easier it was to keep her perspective.

Not that she would have any trouble tonight.

She wouldn't even be touching Josh. It was all about closing her eyes and finding her own pleasure.

The notion followed her into the shower. Her senses came alive as she stood beneath the spray. Warm water sluiced over her skin. She remembered the tickling trickle of brown sugar syrup over her body and the way Josh had savored her with his mouth and his tongue.

And how much she wanted to feel him again.

An orgasm, she reminded herself. *It's not him, in particular, that you're hungry for. It's another mind-blowing orgasm. No man required.* That's what she told herself, but when she retrieved her own vibrator from her lingerie drawer and stretched out on her bed, she found herself missing the brush of chest hair against her nipples and the feel of hard, muscled skin beneath her fingertips. She couldn't seem to lose herself in the cool, vibrating sensation against her clitoris.

Because it was too cool.

She finally gave up and headed down to her kitchen for the leftover Chocolate Orgasm batter sitting in her refrigerator. She'd just retrieved a spoon and taken a mouthwatering bite when her gaze zeroed in on the large box that sat off to the side of her kitchen. Paul and his plastic-wrapped torso sat surrounded by white foam popcorn, his bent legs hooked over the side of the box. They'd been so busy that Sue hadn't had a chance to re-package him.

Holly walked over to the box and pulled the plastic bag from his head. She peeled the tape off his eyes and they opened to reveal a vivid brown gaze that seemed to stare straight through her. She grasped the piece of foam in his mouth and tugged. Sure enough, he had a tongue just as Sue had said. And soft lips. Not kissable, mind you. But still soft. She could see how some women might get into a little lip-lock with him.

But Holly needed more than a kiss at the moment. She needed warm skin and a hair-roughened chest and an orgasm. And she needed it in the next half hour.

She set her spoon on a nearby counter, grasped Paul under his arms and pulled him from the box. He was firm, but not heavy, and she managed to transfer him to a chair with minimal effort. Grabbing a pair of scissors from a nearby drawer, she cut through the remaining tape and plastic until Paul looked like any other naked blonde who might happen to be sitting at her table.

Her gaze traveled over his broad shoulders and six-pack abs to the impressive package in his lap. Before she could stop herself, she leaned over and touched him. Sure enough, the heat from her fingertips worked its magic. His member twitched and expanded just a fraction. She touched him again, stroking from root to tip. He grew hard and literally throbbed beneath her fingertips. She pressed a pressure point on his chest and his member started to vibrate.

Need tightened in her belly, but not because of the transformation happening right before her. Rather, she thought of Josh and the way he'd responded to her touch. He'd come alive and then he'd brought her alive and then *bam!*

She blew out a deep breath and tried to calm her suddenly pounding heart.

Don't even think it, a voice whispered as she stared at Paul. *It's a sex doll, for heaven's sake. You can't have an orgasm with a sex doll.*

At the same time, Holly wasn't a hypocrite. Like a lot

of healthy women her age, she had a vibrator. The penis between Paul's legs was exactly that. A super deluxe vibrator that had three adjustable speeds. And just happened to be attached to a body and a face that, while man-made, looked as good if not better than the real thing.

Sort of.

He wasn't even close to Josh McGraw and his dark good looks and sinful charm. But then, that was the whole point. To have a mind-blowing orgasm *without* Josh.

Which was exactly what she intended to do.

"*WHAT THE HELL?*"

Josh watched from the doorway as Holly straddled the man who sat in the kitchen chair and his gut twisted. Christ, she was going for it right here and now with another...

The thought faded as several things seemed to register: 1) the man's arms didn't move, 2) his hands didn't slide around her to cup her buttocks and anchor her in place and, 3) he didn't buck and thrust his pelvis toward her.

No normal, red-blooded man could *not* react to a woman like Holly.

His gaze swiveled to the gigantic cardboard box sitting off to the side. Chunks of foam and pieces of plastic wrapping littered the floor. *Warm Bodies*. The name registered and he remembered an ad from some men's magazine.

A doll. The man was a *doll,* for chrissake!

The truth hit him and he expected to feel a measure of relief. No such luck. While she wasn't getting busy with someone else, she still wasn't getting busy with him.

At the same time, he couldn't seem to find his voice to put a stop to it. Instead, he watched as she sat astride the seated man, braced her hands on his shoulders, threw her head back and started to ride him. Her back arched and her full lips parted. Her soft, round breasts trembled as she lifted and slid back down. Her nipples hardened into rosy, ripe points and Josh swallowed.

He wasn't sure what he hated the most—the fact that she was enjoying herself without him or the fact that he couldn't seem to tear his eyes away from the sight.

And so he watched for the next several moments, until he grew so hard that he had to lock his knees to keep from falling. Her lips trembled around a sigh and the sound thrummed through his body. His testicles throbbed and his gut ached and he stepped farther into the room.

The urge to pull her away from the doll, throw her to the floor and give it to her until she forgot about everything and everyone drove him across the room.

He took the last step and grabbed her arm. Her eyes popped open and she stared up at him with a startled expression.

"What are you doing here?" she blurted. Her shocked gaze swiveled to the wall clock. "You're forty-five minutes early."

What *was* he doing? Getting jealous and crazed over a woman when Josh McGraw never got jealous and crazed over any woman. It just didn't happen. Not now. Not ever. *Control.*

Josh forced aside the strange emotions warring inside him and focused on the heat in his groin and the desire making his skin tight. He let go of her long enough to pull off his boots.

She stared at him a moment longer before she seemed to realize that she was buck-naked and still sitting astride the doll. "I wa-wa-wasn't," she stammered as she went to climb off. "That is, I was, but I didn't know you would be here early and so I just thought—"

He leaned down, silenced her with his mouth and urged her back down onto the doll. He swallowed her gasp as she sank onto the vibrator and his gut clenched. He deepened the kiss, forcing her mouth open wider, plundering her until the taste and scent of her consumed his senses. Desire burned through him, hotter and brighter than his anger.

He'd already pulled his shirt over his head and reached for the waistband of his jeans by the time she recovered from the kiss. Her eyelids fluttered open just in time to see him push his jeans and underwear down his hips.

"What are you doing?"

"Recipe six." He kicked his jeans and underwear free. His erection bobbed forward, desperate and eager to be touched.

"But we can't." Panic filled her expression. "I mean, we can't. Not yet. We're not upstairs and we don't have everything we need and—"

He kissed her again, hard and rough and quick before pulling back. "Trust me, cupcake. We've got more than we need." And then he dropped to his knees behind her and pressed his lips between her shoulder blades.

"But we're supposed to follow the directions and do it right."

"We'll do it right," he promised as he pulled her back up against his chest and slid his hands around her waist to finger her nipples.

"But we need a bed—*ahhh...*" Her protest faded into a deep, throaty moan that made his cock twitch.

He trailed his hand down her bare stomach until he reached her thin strip of pubic hair. She caught his wrist with desperate fingers.

"Don't."

He nuzzled the soft flesh near her ear. "*Don't* because you don't want me to or because you're embarrassed?"

"I don't..." She caught her lip as if rethinking her answer. "I'm embarrassed," she finally admitted. "I've never masturbated in front of a man, and certainly not with another... I mean, this is the first time I've used one of these."

Joy rushed through him, followed by a wave of desire so intense that it made his teeth ache. "You're so sexy, Holly. Don't ever be embarrassed about that. I love watching you, but I want to feel you, too. *Please.*"

Her hand hesitated on his for a brief moment before her grip loosened. He traced the fine line of silk down to where her slick folds stretched over the vibrator. He traced her tight lips and felt her shudder until his fingers were slick with her moisture.

"Move for me," he murmured as he slid his hands around to stroke her soft, round ass.

Her movements were slow and hesitant at first. She shimmied her hips, moving a little to the right, then to the left until a soft gasp parted her lips.

"That's it, baby." He slid his erection between her buttocks, back and forth, as she worked herself on the vibrator. The slickness trickled from her body, wetting the head of his cock where it nestled in the space between her ass cheeks and the chair beneath her. It was all he could do not to explode right then and there.

But he wanted to watch her go over the edge first. Hear her. Feel her. Then he could let himself go. He concentrated on pushing her higher with his hands and his mouth until she moved faster, her movements desperate, her body deliciously wet and hot.

When Josh slid his hands down Holly's quivering belly and his callused finger touched her clitoris, sharp, sweet pleasure exploded inside her.

She fought to draw air into her lungs as her body hummed with the wondrous sensation of being filled with the vibrator—now on ultraspeed—and surrounded by Josh McGraw.

His hard, muscular arms held her tight. His hot penis nestled between her buttocks. His warm breath stirred the hair on the back of her neck. His musky scent filled her nostrils. His heart hammered against her back.

"I can feel you tighten around the vibrator," Josh murmured against the damp skin of her shoulder. "Every time I stroke you here—" he pinched her clitoris ever so lightly "—you tighten around *him*. You like feeling us both, don't you?"

I like you.

The words were there, but she didn't say them. Because she knew, despite the strange tenderness in her chest, that she didn't really mean them. It was the heat of the moment smothering her common sense. She didn't like *him*. She liked what he was doing with his hands. She liked the vibrator humming inside her. She liked the dual sensation.

At least that's what she told herself as she closed her eyes and arched back against him.

He didn't ask any more questions. He answered her unspoken request and fingered her clit, rubbing and circling the nub until her vision blurred and she couldn't seem to catch her breath. He stirred a pleasure so fierce that she thought she might explode.

And then she did.

Heat swept her from the soles of her feet to the roots of her hair, setting ablaze everything in between including the notion that the second bite was never quite as good as the first. It was better. And so was the third.

She braced her hands against the doll's shoulders, her fingers digging into his flesh as her body shook with convulsions.

Through the ringing in her ears, she heard Josh's deep groan as he spilled himself against her bottom, followed by a string of curse words that would have made her ears burn if her entire body hadn't already gone up in smoke. His arms slid around her and he held her close against him for the next few moments, as if he never meant to let her go.

As if.

If there was one thing Holly knew, it was that Josh McGraw fully intended to turn her loose. Just as she fully intended to do the same.

Her arms curled around his forearms, her hands closed over his and she held tight.

But not yet. Not just yet.

10

JOSH AIMED the blue flame and sliced through the last layer of tangled metal before killing the power on the portable welding torch. He pulled off his goggles and gloves and grabbed a small crowbar. Shoving the edge of the tool beneath what was left of the transmission, he pried the part loose and pulled it free of the engine hull.

Holly had been right, he thought as he set the part off to the side and reached for the new transmission he'd ordered online from the small parts dealer that supplied his charter company.

There *were* similar parts between a car and a plane. Plugs, shocks, fuel pumps, fan belts and a dozen other common items. Granted, the sizes differed dramatically and a plane had more specialized components, but his Cessna still required the same basics as the ancient GTO.

He grabbed his drill and bolted the new transmission into position. It was his last major fix before moving on to the bodywork, and at the pace he was going, he would be finished with the restoration in no time.

He finished with the last bolt and pushed and pulled to make sure the connection was secure. He leaned back and wiped a hand over his sweaty brow. It was the dead of night and the temperature had dropped a few degrees, but not nearly enough to cool the heat swamping his senses. The extra shop lights he'd set up off to the side pushed back the darkness and made the barn that much hotter.

Grabbing a nearby glass of watered-down iced tea, he downed half the contents. The liquid cooled his throat and the caffeine sent a jolt to his brain.

Not that he needed it. It was well after midnight and he was still wide-awake.

He couldn't blame Uncle Eustace and Aunt Lurline. While they fought about everything from how he liked his eggs in the morning, to who she thought was more handsome—David Letterman or Conan O'Brien— Josh had started tuning them out days ago. He was either too busy to let the bickering get to him—he spent his mornings on the back of a horse, overseeing the various activities on the ranch, his afternoons in front of a computer screen working on the financial end of the Iron Horse—or too preoccupied thinking about Holly.

It was the thinking that drove him out to the barn and under the hood of the GTO. Only when he picked up a tool and focused his attention on the engine could he forget the fact that her scent seemed to linger longer than any other woman's, and her voice still echoed in his ears and her image stayed vivid in his head long after it should have faded.

He was definitely losing it. But at least he had the GTO to keep him just this side of a straitjacket and save him from his damnable thoughts.

Just the way he'd had old Mr. Baines and his crop

duster to salvage his sanity so long ago when his parents had died and his grandfather had pushed him away.

I guess we all gravitate toward the familiar.

She'd been right, all right.

While crop dusting had been a world away from hauling ass down Main Street in a souped-up muscle car, the rush had been the same. He'd felt free and in control and lost in the moment. When he'd climbed into the copilot's seat of the crop duster, there'd been no worries, no fear, no regret. It had been the only time he didn't think about his past and the night he'd lied to his mother.

And so he walked out to the barn night after night, so that he wouldn't have to think now. Not about Holly or the fact that while he'd managed to piece most of the ranch back together, the Iron Horse would never be completely whole without those last twenty-five acres that Holly still refused to sell him.

Close, but not quite there.

That's what ate at his gut so damned often now and made him feel even more unsettled. Restless. *Incomplete.*

The missing land.

That's what Josh told himself. He just wasn't so sure he believed it anymore.

"I FEEL A LITTLE funny about this." Holly eyeballed the bread sticks piled on her plate. It was Monday night and she had accompanied Sue to the Elk's monthly spaghetti dinner.

"Now, but once the ladies' bible study lets out and this place really fills up, you'll be thanking me." Sue retrieved another fresh-baked goody and topped off Holly's pile before filling her own plate. "I'm telling you, these things are like gold. It's Irma Bushnell's special recipe—she's married to Sonny who's the Elk in charge of activities. The woman's been an annual Romeo Bake-Off champion at least a dozen times." Sue took a bite and closed her eyes in ecstasy. "She's got a gift," she declared after savoring her mouthful.

"It's the flour," Holly said after she'd eaten a few bites of her own. "She goes strictly for the baking flour and does extracareful sifting." When Sue raised her eyebrows, Holly added, "That's what gives them the melt-in-your-mouth texture."

"You're good."

Holly grinned. "So are these." She turned back to the buffet. "Should we stockpile the meatballs, too?" Sue stopped her just shy of the serving tongs and shook her head.

"Francis Marbury does the meatballs," Sue said.

"And?"

"Francis *Marbury,* as in Marbury Grain and Feed."

"And?"

"Word has it that Marbury Grain and Feed places the biggest Purina Dog Chow order in the county."

"So?"

Sue shrugged. "All's I'm saying is that it's mighty suspicious. And speaking of suspicious, I still can't believe that Paul actually caught fire and melted."

"We shouldn't have left the box so close to the oven." Holly averted her gaze and stepped toward the mountain of noodles.

"But he was on the opposite side of the room."

"It's a commercial oven. It gets really hot. And with this heat wave…I've felt like melting myself a time or two."

"But he was supposed to be antiflammable."

"Maybe he had a defect." Before Sue could think on the subject, Holly rushed on, "At least the company is making good on their guarantee and sending you a brand-new doll."

"But shouldn't I have to send back the damaged one so they can test it and figure out what went wrong?"

"Ordinarily, but it went up in flames so fast that the only thing left were a few metal pieces which were little more than junk." Or at least that's what Holly figured would be left if Paul had actually met his maker rather than the inside of her attic where she'd hidden him away after recipe number six. She couldn't very well let Sue ship back used goods and so she'd stashed Paul, invented the oven story and ordered Sue a brand-new doll. "I can't wait to see the cowboy doll. You say he actually looks like Bert Wayne?"

"Sort of, but he's not nearly as handsome. Bert has these incredible eyes…"

The mention of Sue's ex effectively changed the topic until Sue spotted the man himself and headed across the room to flaunt her new makeover. Meanwhile, Holly made her way over to a small table. It was early, but there were already a lot of people. Apparently, Sue had been right about the breadsticks because she saw several other people with their plates piled high. She was just about to eat one herself when she heard a voice behind her.

"You must be new to town."

She turned to see a man with dark hair and a wide smile standing behind her. He looked to be about her age, his eyes a deep, warm brown that crinkled when he smiled.

"As a matter of fact, I am."

His smile widened. "Dime Jackson's the name." He held out his hand and she hesitated.

Hello? The guy wants to shake your hand, not toss you over his shoulder and carry you to bed. And even if he did want to carry you to bed, what's so wrong with that?

She thought of Josh and their last encounter. And the fact that they were going to have two more—provided she could figure out the house special. She wasn't the type of woman to juggle two men at one time.

You don't have to juggle. Just keep your eyes open for future prospects. Relax. Open up. Make friends.

Holly smiled and placed her hand in his.

"...SO I TRIED my jumper cables, but the blasted things didn't do nothin' but scare the living daylights out of me." Davy Crockett Buckhorn took a sip of his iced tea and leaned back in his chair. At ninety-two, he was the oldest of the four brothers sitting around the small card table and the oldest official Elk in the entire county. An honor once held by Josh's grandfather who'd been ninety-three when he'd passed away last year.

"Why, I nearly peed myself when the jolt hit me," he went on. "There was this *zap,* and *bam,* I was seeing Jesus. It was one of them near-death experiences like they talk about on the TV."

"It's the cotton pickin' truth and nothin' but the truth," said the man to Davy's right. Jim Bowie Buckhorn had just turned ninety, which made him the second oldest of the bunch.

"You can say that again."

"Damn straight."

The comments came from the other two men at the table. Sam Houston Buckhorn was eighty-seven and his baby brother, Stephen Austin, was eighty-four.

While all four men were too old to do little more than sip tea and gossip, they'd been the county's biggest hell-raisers back in the day, and his grandfather's closest friends. Permanent fixtures at the Iron Horse when Josh had been growing up. Always sitting out on the porch, playing dominoes or cards or just shooting the shit till daybreak.

Josh had always been right in the middle of it all. He'd been just a kid, maybe six years old when he'd left his brothers sound asleep and tiptoed down the stairs on a Friday night to ease open the front door and listen in on the men's good time. He'd been eight when his gramps had first caught a glimpse of him and asked him to fetch a plate of sandwiches from the kitchen. He'd brought out the platter and stuck around to nibble corn nuts and watch. For the next five years, he'd thrived on the wild stories they'd told and watched in awe as they'd played high-stakes poker. He'd learned the difference between a flush and a full house, heard the first of many dirty jokes and discovered the various pleasures to be had with a woman.

Any and every woman.

At the time, he hadn't really thought about the right and wrong of everything he'd heard—each member of the group had been married. Josh had been young. Impressionable. A full-blooded McGraw. And so the men's lives had sounded so exciting that he'd simply lived for the day when he could join in and tell some stories of his own. Until he'd turned sixteen. He'd changed his mind then, but it had been too late.

He'd already turned into one of them and he'd proven it the night of his mother's death when he'd covered for his father.

Surprisingly, the thought didn't leave near the bad taste in his mouth that it usually did. He still felt the tightness in his throat and the pain in his chest, but it seemed softer. As if it had faded, just like the men in front of him.

Josh turned his attention to Davy. Gone was the loud, obnoxious flirt who'd once bragged that he'd taken on four women at the same time. In his place sat an old, hunched-over man who could barely get his twisted fingers around the tea glass because of the rheumatoid arthritis that had devastated his body.

"So's then I tried to check the fan belt. But my screwdriver kept slipping and I stabbed the dad-burned oil pan and gave it a good dent. Damned old hands. Getting old is hell."

"It's worse than hell. It's like never-ending Sunday dinner with your momma-in-law," Jim added.

"You can say that again," Sam chimed in.

"Damn straight," said Stephen.

Davy shook his snow-white head. "I finally worked

the fan belt off and replaced it, but she still wouldn't even turn over, so's I had no choice but to call a wrecker and have her hauled over to Shake McCauley's for a look-see. If anybody can fix it, I figure it'll be Shake. Shake's about the best mechanic in town."

"Forget the town. Shake's the best in the whole danged county."

"You can say that again."

"Damn straight."

The band launched into a familiar Toby Keith song and the dance floor filled with people. Josh's gaze shifted to Holly in time to see her shake hands with Dime Jackson.

"Isn't Shake the *only* mechanic in town?" Josh asked, forcing his gaze back to the old men. It wasn't like Josh had any real claim on Holly.

Sure, they were having sex, but that was purely physical. It wasn't as if he *cared* whether or not she talked to other men.

"Been the only one around here who can crawl an engine since your daddy passed on way back when. Your grandpa knew his stuff, but he couldn't get around too well these last years on account of his bad knees. And then he had the tremors 'cause of all that high blood pressure. So Shake's all we got, and that ain't sayin' much considerin' he spent five hours under the hood of my old Lincoln and he still couldn't figure out what was wrong with her."

Out of the corner of his eye, Josh saw Dime smile at Holly, and she smiled at him, and something twisted in Josh's gut. His mind rushed back to last Saturday night. He'd felt the same stab of jealousy when he'd seen her with the doll, but it had been nothing compared to the slicing and dicing he felt right now.

His mouth drew into a thin line as he shifted his attention back to the old men.

Okay, so he cared.

She was a beautiful woman and she had a good heart. He admired her determination to make a new life and the strength it took to hold her own while the town treated her like an outsider.

Hell, he actually *liked* her.

While their relationship might be purely business, and very temporary, he wanted exclusives with her for the time being.

"So where's the Lincoln now?" Josh asked.

"Had it towed back to my place. I ordered me some of them *Time Life* books off the TV. The ones that give you step-by-step instructions on how to fix stuff. I figure I'll read up and fix it myself. I was wonderin' if I could borrow your daddy's old tools. Never was into cars myself and so I don't have a very good collection."

"Sure." Josh eyeballed Dime who left Holly to climb onto the stage and make a song dedication to the new lady in town. The band struck up an old Hank Williams tune and Josh frowned.

"…used to know my way around an engine pretty well in my day, if I do say so myself. I know I can fix whatever ails her if I can just get a good look-see."

Josh's gaze went to Jim and his thick bifocals before dropping to the twisted hand resting on his knee. "How about if I drop by the house and help you take a look?"

"I thought you gave up car engines for that fancy-pants flying?"

"I do charter flights. Very few passengers and no crew. When things go wrong, I fix it myself. I still know my way around an engine. You fellas take care," Josh said as he started to turn.

"You ain't gonna play dominoes with us?" Davy asked.

"Not tonight." Tonight, Josh was playing with someone else.

And the game started now.

"HE'S NOT YOUR TYPE." Josh's deep, husky words slid into Holly's ears and prickled the hair on the nape of her neck. Awareness raced up her spine and kick-started her heartbeat.

Not here, a voice whispered. *Not now. Not him.*

"I don't know about that. I could get used to a man singing me songs."

"If the man could sing."

Dime Jackson hit a high note and she tried not to cringe. "It's still sweet."

"Too sweet," Josh said, his warmth cradling her back. He didn't actually touch her, but it didn't matter. He stood so close she could smell the clean scent of his aftershave.

"Sweet can be good."

"Sweet doesn't make you catch your breath." He leaned in closer and she felt his lips graze her temple. "It doesn't make your stomach do flips, and it doesn't make your skin hot and tight. It doesn't turn you on."

"Maybe I'm after more than a quick turn-on. Maybe I want something solid and lasting and long-term." She smiled, determined to focus on the thought rather than the awful voice blasting from the speakers.

"All the more reason to avoid sweet," Josh said after a few hair-raising lyrics. "Sweet equals damned frustrating when you're talking long-term."

She started to argue, but then she had a sudden glimpse of herself as an old woman sitting in the Elk's Lodge, listening to Dime butcher "Walking the Floor Over You" for the thousandth time.

Her smile disappeared and her gaze shifted around the room.

"What about him?" She pointed to a nice-looking cowboy standing at the punch bowl. He ladled a cup and handed it to an elderly woman standing nearby. "He seems nice. Nice is always good when you're talking long-term."

"If you're his mother."

"That's his mother?" She watched as he helped the woman to a nearby table and steered her into a seat, before turning to fetch a plate of spaghetti.

"And his date."

A momma's boy she didn't need.

"How about him?" She pointed to the blond cowboy who toted a large pan of lasagna. He nodded to several people as he headed for the buffet and added the steaming pan to the long table. "He's good-looking. He's got a great smile. He's obviously not afraid to help out in the kitchen. That definitely says hot prospect."

"Seems like you're not the only person who thinks so." Josh pointed to the large man sitting behind the ticket counter. The ticket guy glanced over at the spaghetti-toting cowboy and winked. Mr. Hot Prospect winked back before turning to saunter toward the kitchen.

A surge of relief went through her and she stiffened.

Hello? You're supposed to be disappointed when an attractive prospect gets eliminated.

She knew that, but with Josh standing so close and her heartbeat thundering so loudly in her ears, she was hard-pressed to remember the ingredients to her prize-winning Cherry Body Bon Bons, much less her vow to find Mr. Long-Term. At the moment, it was Mr. Short-Term who seemed much more interesting.

She drew a shaky breath, gathered her control and directed her attention across the room. "How about that one?" She pointed to a distinguished-looking man wearing a silver-belly Stetson, a starched white shirt and crisp jeans. A few silvery strands threaded through his dark hair. "He looks like a younger version of Sean Connery."

"Thanks to a bottle of Clairol. He's this close to ordering off the senior citizen's menu over at Waffle World."

"Older men are distinguished."

"At first, but then the arthritis gets the best of them and before you know it, you're ordering Ben-Gay by the case. He's definitely too old for you."

"And that one?" She pointed to another man who stood in the corner laughing it up with his buddies.

"Too loud."

"And that one?"

"Too strange."

"What about—"

"Too ugly," he told her before she could even finish her question.

"Okay, fine." She blew out an exasperated breath. "So which one *is* my type?"

"Let's see." His deep, husky voice lowered a notch as he leaned closer. The warmth of his body seeped through her cotton tank top and warmed her skin. "A woman like you needs a man who'll appreciate her. Someone who likes home cooking."

"Not all cooking," she murmured. "I only do desserts."

"A man with a sweet tooth," he corrected. "A good-looking man with a sweet tooth."

"I like good-looking."

"And strong. An independent woman needs a strong man, otherwise, she'll wind up pushing him around. A wimp is fine at first—women like a man who caters to her every whim—but it gets old pretty quick and kills the attraction, which means you can forget long-term. I haven't met a woman yet who gets hot and bothered over a pushover."

"True. At the same time, he can't be overbearing. He needs to be strong, but not too strong."

"Just strong enough to take the upper hand when necessary."

"When I want him to."

"When you need him to." He pulled her into a dark corner of the room, nuzzling her ear, his soft breath stirring the hair at her temple, his chest brushing her back. "Someone who can cut through all the formality and get straight to the point. Someone who isn't afraid to go after what he wants when he wants it." His lips touched her neck. "Like me." He slid a strong hand around her waist. His fingertips found their way beneath the hem of her tank top and grazed her bare skin. "Like now."

She meant to step forward and break the contact. She really did. She'd promised herself to keep their association strictly business—the sex restricted to the right time, the right place—and to open herself up to a real relationship. One that went beyond the usual, safe, three-month mark. The kind that didn't hinge on lust, but friendship. Respect. Genuine *like*.

She knew that, but with the darkness enveloping her and the slow, sweet country song filling her ears and thrumming through her body, she was having a very hard time keeping her priorities straight.

Relationship. Sex.

Sex. Relationship.

Relationship. Sex.

Then again, maybe it was his hands—so strong and warm and overwhelming—that melted her resolve completely.

His thumb traced a lazy circle a few inches beneath her breast and her knees trembled. It was definitely the hands.

"You need a man who knows how much you like this." His touch moved higher, trailing the underside of her breast before slipping over her bra to the lace that covered her nipple. "A man who knows how much you like being touched here. Like this." He fingered the ripe bud before catching it between his thumb and forefinger and tugging until her breath caught.

"It's not just about sex," she said, slightly breathless. "I want more. I want a future."

"But do you want it more than this?"

She didn't. At that moment, the only thing she wanted was Josh McGraw over her. Inside her. Again.

The realization sent a bolt of panic through her and she stiffened. "This isn't the right time for this. We have a deal."

"We *had* a deal. What we've got right now... Hell, I'm not sure what we have except that it's a lot more intense than anything I've ever felt before. It's more than business between us, Holly. You know it, you just won't admit it. Not yet."

"Not ever. When I give my word, I keep it. No strings attached. No deviating from the schedule."

"I can't see you and not want you, Holly. Hell, I want you even before I see you, whether it's Saturday and I'm thinking about the night ahead, or Monday when I'm sitting across from you at a chamber of commerce meeting. I want you the same. Regardless of the time or place. When you're in the same room with me—" his hand tightened on her waist for emphasis "—it's all I can do not to push you up against the nearest wall and plunge into your soft, sweet body."

"Don't—"

"I can barely control myself, and I know you feel the same."

"It doesn't matter. It's not part of the—"

"—deal," he finished for her. "I know that, but I can't help the way I feel any more than you can help the way you feel. I see your lips tremble when I get a little too close. I feel your body shiver and your muscles tense as if you can barely keep from reaching out." He dropped his hand then, his fingers grazing the vee between her legs.

Heat speared her and her legs quivered.

"You want me, right here and right now, because we're good together."

"We want different things."

"Right now we want the same thing." His voice lowered. "Stop fighting, Holly. Let's enjoy each other for the time being."

But she didn't want to enjoy him *for the time being*. She wanted forever.

Not with him, mind you. She knew Josh was as temporary as she'd always been. But with someone. A man she could laugh with, grow old with, love.

She wasn't in love with Josh.

Not yet.

She forced aside the last thought. "I really have to go."

"You *have* to or you *want* to?"

"What does it matter?"

"It doesn't." But she knew from the sudden desperation in his gaze that it mattered a great deal. As if he needed to know if she was doing her best to resist the attraction, or if she simply wasn't that attracted in the first place.

The answer was there on the tip of her tongue. "I *want* to leave." That's all she had to say to put things in the proper perspective between them and make it crystal clear that he was wrong. That their relationship wasn't anything out of the ordinary as far as she was concerned. No inexplicable intensity. No heightened level of desire. Nothing special.

"I need to go," she murmured, and then she turned and walked away before she completely lost her head and kissed him just because she wanted to.

No. She wasn't giving in. She'd had far too much practice at holding her emotions in check to let loose now. Sure, she'd done it in the past because she'd been the one leaving, the one hesitant to get involved when now it was Josh who couldn't commit to a relationship. But the principle was the same—control.

She'd perfected it over the years and it was simply a matter of practicing it until their arrangement was over and Josh went back to his life.

That's what she told herself. Unfortunately, the notion made her more depressed than relieved. As much as Holly hated to admit it to herself, she didn't just need Josh Mc-Graw to help prepare for the luncheon with the Juliets.

She wanted him.

More than she'd ever wanted any other man in her life.

"IT'S COMPLETELY lactose free," Holly told Old Duke the next morning when she stopped by his place on her way to nearby Cherryville to ship her orders. She held up the white box. "I used special ingredients."

Old Duke lifted the lid and eyeballed the contents before shaking his head. "It's got strawberries. Strawberries break my boy out something terrible. *Everybody* knows that." Old Duke pushed his glasses up and gazed at her. "So how long did you say you was in town for?"

Holly gave him her best smile. "I live here now."

"Do tell? Where'd you say you was from again? Harrisburg? Hamlet?"

"Houston."

He made a face. "Now that's a shame. Got me a second cousin over in Hamlet, and a great-nephew over in Harrisburg. Nice little towns." He shook his head. "Cain't say the same for Houston, though. Never did like those Rockets much. The San Antonio Spurs... Now there's a basketball team. Talented bunch of fellers, and close to home, too."

Holly blew out a disappointed breath and started to turn. "Sorry to bother you."

"Hold up, there." Old Duke reached for the box and whisked it out of her hands. "We all make mistakes. You don't fret over it. Just run on along and I'll take care of this for you."

"Sassy and Frassy again?"

"Damn straight." He smiled. "Those gals will eat anything."

"YOU'RE NOT SUPPOSED to be here," Holly told Josh when she opened the door to find him standing on her doorstep the following evening. "It's *Tuesday.*"

He grinned and winked. "Then I'm right on time."

She shook her head. "We're not meeting tonight. I'm hosting the car wash committee. We're painting signs tonight."

"What do you know?" His grin widened as he pulled a paintbrush out of his back pocket. "I'm a member of that committee."

"Since when?"

"Since about one o'clock this afternoon. I ran into Stewart at the diner and he mentioned that he still needed volunteers." When she frowned, he added, "Don't get yourself all worked up, cupcake." He stepped toward her, backing her up into the foyer as he walked inside. "My being here doesn't violate our agreement." Just before he moved past her, he leaned down, his lips grazing her ear. "We're not having sex."

Technically, he was right.

Holly held tight to the thought for the next few hours as she served refreshments, helped with the dozen signs needed to advertise Friday's fund-raiser and tried to ignore Josh and his smile.

Impossible. He was there every time she turned around. He followed her into the kitchen and helped her carry the cheese and crackers. He helped her spread newspapers throughout the living room to catch any spilled paint. He popped open cans of paint and carried the finished signs out onto the front porch to dry.

After everyone left, he even lingered to help her clean up the mess.

"You really don't have to stay." Holly pressed a lid onto what was left of a can of orange paint.

"I don't mind." He set the lid on a quart of robin-egg blue and hammered it down.

"Even so, you don't have to. I'm sure you've got lots of other, more important things to do."

"Like play referee for my great-aunt Lurline and my great-uncle Eustace?" He shook his head. "Trust me, clean-up duty is a hell of a lot better."

"I was thinking more important, as in cattle to tend and supplies to order and other general ranch stuff."

She eyed him as he hammered down the lid on a can of hot pink and her mind raced with questions.

Of course, she wasn't going to ask any of them. The less she knew about him the better.

Then again, if she knew more, maybe she wouldn't wonder so much and then she could stop thinking about him.

It was a weak argument, but it won with all the heat and testosterone smothering her common sense. That and the fact that it only seemed natural to talk to him. He *was* her neighbor, albeit temporary.

"So your great-aunt and -uncle live at the Iron Horse?"

He nodded. "For the past five years. They moved in when my grandfather found out that he had prostate cancer. Aunt Lurline wanted to take care of him—she was his only sister. Since she and Uncle Eustace lived on their own spread a good forty miles away and they don't like to drive—they're in their late eighties and they've got cataracts—they thought it would be easier just to move. They sold the place, distributed the proceeds between eight kids and headed for the Iron Horse."

"So what are they going to do now that your grandfather's gone?"

"Nothing. It's their home now. The house is big enough for three families, let alone three people. They'll stay on and Mason will keep an eye on them."

"And play referee?"

He grinned and reached for the last can of paint. "They argue a lot."

"What about?"

"Anything. Everything."

"So you're not really here to help. You're here to hide."

"That's half the reason."

"And the other half?"

He eyed her and she had the strange feeling he was asking himself the very same question. "Have you sized up any more relationship prospects?"

"You pretty much eliminated most of the single men in town last night."

"There were a few that didn't make it to the dinner."

"I'm talking living, breathing, viable options."

He grinned. "So am I."

"Like who?"

He shrugged. "There's Slim Collier. James Pitt. Scooter Perkins."

Holly shook her head. "First off, Slim Collier is divorced from Mabel, who's a jealous nut. I don't need to find any dead rabbits in my oven. James Pitt is even worse because he's the jealous nut. He beat up a guy just for saying 'excuse me' to his last date. As for Scooter Perkins, he's like a hundred years old and the oldest citizen in Romeo."

He let loose a low whistle. "You've been doing your homework."

"Sue filled me in on the first two. I ran into Scooter—literally—at the Food-o-rama when he was buying denture cream. I accidentally hit him with my backside. I said I was sorry and he said, "Hi, there. I'm Scooter." She did her best Southern drawl. "I'm the oldest SOB around these-here parts."

Josh grinned. "He's a proud man."

Her own smile faded as she eyed him. "What about you?"

"What do you mean?"

"You and your brothers own the largest ranch for hundreds of miles. Your ancestors founded this town. You ought to be just as puffed up as Scooter, yet all you want is to walk away from here. I can't help but wonder why."

"I have a business in Arizona."

"A charter business that you run single-handedly. An apartment you're obviously too busy to live in. No significant other. Nothing *really* pulling you away. Most of the family you have left are right here. It makes sense that you would settle down in Romeo."

"I like my own space."

"Obviously. But you still haven't answered my question." Her gaze met his. "Why?"

He stared at her a long moment before he finally shook his head and shrugged. "I guess old habits die hard."

"Meaning?"

"When my folks died, it was really hard on my grandfather. My dad was his only child. Seeing me and my brothers day in and day out only made it that much harder, so he pushed us away. He didn't want us helping him around the ranch like we usually did. Hell, he could barely tolerate to look at us over the dinner table. The less time we spent at home, the better."

"That must have been hard."

It *had* been hard, which was why Josh didn't like to think about it, much less talk about the subject. He hadn't just lost his parents. He'd lost his home. His grandfather. *Everything*. But for some reason, saying the words now, to Holly, didn't make his gut ache.

"Rance started sleeping over at his coach's house," he went on, "and spending every waking moment on the football field. Mason entered any and every rodeo that took him out of town when he wasn't in school or practicing at a nearby ranch. I got an after-school job at the Baines's farm on the other side of town. Mr. Baines did his own crop dusting. That's where I first started flying. When we graduated, Rance went off to play for Texas A & M, Mason left to rodeo full-time and I headed for Austin to get my pilot's license. We've been gone ever since."

"Until now."

"Actually, until about four years ago. When my grandfather found out about his prostate cancer, he tracked us down and apologized. We've been home off and on since then."

"He's lucky you forgave him."

"There wasn't anything to really forgive. We stayed away because he wanted us to, not because we were pissed off. We know he had his reasons. Christ, he'd just lost the closest person to him."

"You lost, too." The fierce way she jumped to Josh's defense stirred a warmth in his chest. "You lost a mother and a father, and you didn't turn your back on anyone."

"No, but I turned my back on this town." He was still turning his back. Still walking away from his past and trying to stay one step ahead of the guilt that dogged him. "The same way I turned my back on my mother when I lied to her."

"You were just a kid and you were scared."

"I should have told her the truth."

"Yes, but it still wouldn't have changed what happened. She would have still died and your father would have still reacted the same way when he found out."

"Guilty as charged."

"Maybe." Silence settled between them for a long moment before she added, "But maybe it wasn't guilt that sent your father off into a tailspin, so much as regret."

"What do you mean?"

"Maybe he loved her and he couldn't stand the thought of living without her. Maybe he didn't want to live without her. I know when my mother died, the thought of waking up and facing the next day on my own scared the hell out of me."

"But you didn't kill yourself."

"I was a kid. I didn't think like that. But if I had been older, I might have considered it."

"My dad wouldn't have cheated on my mother if he'd loved her."

"Maybe he didn't realize the depth of his feelings for her until he lost her. The world is full of people who take things for granted and never really appreciate all that they have until something is taken away. Your father could have been one of them."

"Why are you trying to defend him?"

"I'm not. I'm just saying that things might not be what they seem."

"They're what they seem, all right. You didn't know my father."

"True. But I know you and I know that you're taking full responsibility for something that wasn't your fault. You're not to blame for what your father did or didn't do. You're you, not him."

He'd told himself the same thing so many times, but he'd never quite believed it until Holly Farraday stared into his eyes and said it with such conviction because she truly believed it.

She believed in him.

Not that the realization changed anything.

Josh still intended to fulfill his granddad's dying wish and find some peace for himself in the process. A promise was a promise, and he was close. One more week and two more recipes and he would be that much closer.

The kicker was, he didn't *feel* close.

The realization hit him as he packed up the last of the painting supplies, said good-night to Holly and tried to forget the sincerity in her gaze. As he drove away, his hands itched and his gut twisted and his nerves buzzed.

He felt restless. Anxious. Dissatisfied.

And damned if it wasn't getting worse by the minute.

11

HOLLY STOOD on her front porch early the next morning and watched the familiar red pickup truck barrel down the dirt road in front of her drive. The tires kicked up gravel. A cloud of dust dogged the old truck, the bed piled high with the day's deliveries.

And yesterday's.

She still hadn't received the three sacks of flour, twenty pounds of sugar and four cases of extralarge bakery boxes she'd ordered at the beginning of the week. It wasn't the delivery itself—she could easily have her deliveries shipped to Cherryville. It was what the delivery itself meant.

The engine grumbled and the old truck shifted gears as if to slow. She stepped down off the porch as the truck approached the entrance to her drive. The gears grumbled and the engine sputtered. Hope flowered in her chest only to deflate and sink to the pit of her stomach as the truck rumbled right by headed for the opposite side of the county. Obviously, fattening up Sassy and Frassy wasn't earning her any brownie points. She was still last on the list.

The outsider.

Holly forced aside the thought. She belonged here. She *fit*, at least that's what she told herself as she went about her morning routine. She might have believed it on any ordinary Thursday.

But not the Thursday from hell. It started with her brand-new mixer which started to smoke while mixing the second batch of Caramel Kisses. One minute she was measuring flour for her seductive Cherry Body Bon Bons and the next, she was reaching for the fire extinguisher. By the time she'd put out the small fire, her kitchen looked as if someone had exploded a case of powdered sugar.

"It ain't the mixer," Nick the electrician from Speedy's Electric told her three hours later when he finally arrived. "It's the outlet. It's old and the mixer's new, and the two don't mix 'cause one needs more power than the other can give. See, these old outlets only put out about ten kilowatts per second and most appliances need at least fifteen."

"But it's been working fine."

"That's 'cause there ain't much of a difference between the output and the required input. But the more you use something, the more juice it draws until it just taps out the connection and *bam,* it's fried. That's what you got, little lady. You got a fried connector."

"Can you fix it?"

"Does a bear shit in the woods?"

While Speedy Nick fixed the mixer—a chore that took all afternoon—Holly and Sue cleaned up the kitchen catastrophe and did their best to make up the lost orders. Holly did double duty with a hand-mixer to pick up the slack, until the next disaster struck.

"There's no water," she said when she turned the faucet and heard the rumble and...nothing.

"It might have threw a breaker 'cause of the fire," Nick said. "I'll have a look-see."

The look-see turned into a search-and-destroy machine as Nick went through her entire breaker box, replacing fuses and switches and recutting wires.

"It's the cartridge in the pump itself," he told her several hours later. "It needs to be replaced."

"So replace it."

"I will just as soon as I can get one from my supplier over in Austin. They don't make these much anymore, so I don't keep extras on my truck." He packed up his toolbox.

"You're leaving?"

"Ain't nothing else I can do without a switch. I'll be back tomorrow."

"Tomorrow morning?" She gave him a hopeful smile.

"I'll get on the horn and get the part overnighted. Just as soon as Duke drops it by, I'll head out here and get you all fixed up."

Her smile died, along with her hope. She was out of water. Off her schedule. And with her fate resting in Duke's hands, tomorrow wasn't looking much better.

She tamped down the dread whirling in her stomach. She hadn't worked her way through school and into a successful business by buckling under pressure. She would work around the upset, and so she sent Sue into town to buy out the bottled-water section of the Food-o-rama.

"Here you go." Sue hefted two gallon jugs onto the kitchen table an hour and a half later.

"There's more in the car, right?"

"This was all they had."

"They had an entire shelf of the stuff."

"That was yesterday. But today the high school pep squad had their annual car wash at the gas station on Main Street."

"And?"

"And they tapped out the city's water supply, so everyone's stockpiling drinking water until the levels get back up to normal."

"That's crazy."

"That's a small town. Last year Coach Rooney decided to make the varsity football squad wash down the bleachers after they lost the regional championships. Those boys used so much water that the town was on rations for two weeks. Course, that's nothing compared to the pep squad car wash. They've got Candy Sue Miller—she was last year's rodeo queen and the girl voted Most Likely to Win a Pamela Anderson Look-alike Contest—doing the windshields, so every male within a fifty-mile radius is lined up right about now. The shortage is sure to get worse."

"Why doesn't the mayor put a stop to it? Limit the number of cars or something?"

"Candy Sue is his niece. Besides, it doesn't inconvenience too many folks because most of them have their own water wells, like you. When one goes kaput, the neighbors usually help out each other."

But Holly only had one neighbor and she wasn't about to ask him for help. In fact, she was doing her best to avoid thinking about him entirely and having a face-to-face was completely out of the question.

"We'll make do." Her brain started to race. "I can substitute milk for some of the water requirements and we'll worry about the cleanup later."

Holly spent the rest of the afternoon making up for the morning's lost orders. By the time the last batch had been pulled from the oven and transferred to the cooling room, her shoulders ached with a vengeance and her temples throbbed with a major headache. While she managed to make up for lost time, she'd yet to get her delivery from Duke, and someone had destroyed her garden—

The thought ground to a halt as she stared at the empty stems pushing up from the newly turned soil. There were no blossoms. No leaves. Nothing resembling the numerous flowers she'd planted last week.

She knelt and fingered the freshly clipped stem. "Who would do this?" she murmured, her throat closing around each word.

"Not *who,* sugar. More like *what.*" Josh McGraw's deep voice slid into her ears and sent electricity humming along her nerve endings.

She turned. The last rays of the sun cast an orange glow and illuminated the man who stood on her back porch. He wore a button-up white shirt, the sleeves rolled back to reveal his tanned forearms, worn jeans and boots. But it wasn't his rugged good looks and striking appearance that stalled her heart for a long moment. It was the deep hunger in his blue gaze. And the concern.

The last thought rooted in her head as she turned back to her devastated garden. "An animal did this?"

"Probably several animals." The squeak of boards

sounded as he stepped down off the porch. Several strides and he hunkered down next to her. He fingered a barely visible footprint nearby. "Deer," he told her. "It's been really dry the past few weeks. Without water to keep things green and growing out here—" he motioned to the surrounding trees and pastureland "—they eat up their natural supply pretty fast."

"Deer." She shook her head and stared at the horizon. Sure, she'd seen a few here and there. From a distance. But right in her backyard? She was definitely out of her element.

She didn't have the strength to push the thought aside the way she usually did. She was tired. Tired of fighting. Tired of trying to fit in and failing miserably.

"I should have known better than to waste my time with a garden. I've never had a green thumb." Her gaze met his. "When I was working my way through cooking school in Chicago, I was living in this one-room, hole-in-the-wall apartment down on Sixth Street. It was one of those basement apartments. Very few windows. Just lots of concrete and artificial light. I decided to buy a plant to liven things up. It worked for a few days, but then I was so busy with school and work that I forgot to water it. It shriveled up and died."

"This wasn't your fault. This garden was like candy to a bunch of kids. They couldn't resist."

She pulled a barren stem from the ground and tossed it. "It was a waste of time." Just like her efforts to befriend Duke and get along with the chamber of commerce members and mow a spread that was obviously too big for one woman.

One way-out-of-her-element woman.

"I'm no good at this." The words were out before she could stop them. "I want to be, but I'm not. This isn't me." Her eyes burned and she blinked, determined to focus. "I want it to be. I really do. But it's not."

She wasn't sure what happened in those next few minutes. She just knew that one moment she was staring at the barren garden and then she was crying and then she was burying her face in the crook of Josh's neck while he held her. Comforted her.

"You're trying too hard," he murmured, his large hand trailing up and down her back. "When you want something really bad, sometimes you have to step back and stop pushing. Sometimes you just have to let things happen."

She had the distinct impression he wasn't just talking about her settling down in Romeo.

Her mind rushed back through the previous week. She remembered his seductive words and his hungry kisses and his challenging words.

It's more than business between us. You know it, you just won't admit it. Not yet.

What had felt warm and comforting morphed into hot and stirring as she drew her next breath. His scent filled her head and her heart thrummed. She became acutely aware of his chest cradling hers and his hard thigh braced ever so lightly between her legs.

The urge to press herself close and rub against him hit her hard and fast. His hands burned into the base of her spine and her breath caught. She waited for him to move, to pull her even closer and weaken her determination to keep things strictly business between them.

Oddly enough, she wanted him to push her because she knew she wouldn't resist this time. She didn't have the strength.

She stared into his gaze and licked her lips. He followed the motion and she knew he wanted to kiss her. As much as she wanted him to.

Her lips parted and his lips parted. His breath brushed her mouth and she closed her eyes and—

"There's a water line in this pasture that runs up to the north fence of my property."

She opened her eyes to find him staring down at her, his gaze guarded. "What?"

"I can tie the line into mine and hook you up with some water until your well is up and running." At her questioning expression, he added, "I saw Sue at the Food-o-rama and she told me what happened. So what do you say?"

"Um, thanks. I appreciate it."

He grinned and her heart stalled. "That's what friends are for."

He wasn't her friend. That's what she told herself for the next few days as she went about her daily routine. He was her lover and her business acquaintance and her neighbor. But not her friend.

But when she walked outside Friday afternoon after a grueling day in the kitchen and found him in her garden, she couldn't ignore the truth any longer.

Her gaze hooked on the newly planted leafy bush blooming with lush yellow flowers.

"Esperanza," he told her as he pushed to his feet and pulled off his work gloves. "They give off a particular scent that repels the deer. At least most of the time. If we're stuck in a drought, you might have to use some liquid fence because the animals tend to overlook the smell when their stomachs are grumbling. But for the most part, they'll steer clear of it."

She blinked back the fresh tears that suddenly blinded her, but it was too late.

"Hey, I didn't mean to make you cry. I just wanted you to have your garden."

"Why?" She blinked and fixed her gaze on him. "Why do you care?"

She wanted him to say that he didn't, that he planted gardens for all his neighbors because it was his grandfather's last wish.

"I wanted to see you smile." His voice was low, husky, as if he didn't want to say the words but he couldn't help himself. "I like seeing you smile. Your eyes crinkle at the corners and there's this light…" He shook his head as if he couldn't believe what he'd just said and tossed the gloves to the ground, next to the box of gardening tools. "I know it sounds crazy."

And how. Why, she couldn't care less what he thought about her eyes. She didn't need his compliments. And she certainly didn't need him planting flowers for her or hooking up water lines or comforting her when she cried over a bunch of silly plants or being so…*nice.*

She needed him to be calm, cool and unaffected, so that she could do the same and keep things in perspective.

Temporary, her conscience whispered the way it always did, but the reminder wasn't enough to harden her resolve. Because she knew the connection with Josh was stronger.

She'd always known it, she simply hadn't wanted to admit it because she'd been terrified to feel more for him. They had no future beyond the next few weeks until his brother came home and so he was the wrong man for her. She shouldn't be wasting her time with him. She'd wasted too much time already.

But suddenly the truth didn't scare her half as much as the realization that she might never meet another man like Josh McGraw. He didn't just turn her on physically. He stirred a warmth that seeped through her and filled up all the empty places. He chased away her loneliness and left her feeling whole.

Complete.

For the first time in her life.

A feeling she wanted to savor, even if only for a little while. It wasn't as if she was going to let herself fall completely in love with him. Just a little bit. Just for a little while. So when he did walk away from Romeo, she would have some sweet memories to comfort her during all the long, lonely nights to come.

She held tight to the thought, blinked back her tears and stepped toward him. "It's crazy, all right."

His gaze swiveled toward her. Anger and humiliation fired in his eyes at her words.

"And it's also the sweetest thing that anyone has ever said to me." And then she did the one thing she'd wanted to do since she'd walked into her backyard and seen Josh planting flowers for her. She pushed up on her tiptoes and touched her lips to his.

JOSH KNEW she was going to kiss him a split second before her lips touched his, and so he braced himself. But knowing it and feeling it were two very different things. He meant to keep his hands to himself and let her make the first move. And the second. And even the third. He wanted to be sure that she wanted him on the same primitive level that he wanted her. With the same intensity. He wanted her to be sure.

Slow. That's what he told himself. He was going to take things slow and easy.

If only his body would cooperate. Instead, his blood raced faster than a Cessna engine readying for takeoff. And there was nothing easy about the erection pressing tight against his jeans.

He shouldn't kiss her back.

He did.

He slid an arm around her and pulled her close. Slanting her head, he deepened the kiss. His lips ate at hers and his tongue tangled with hers and he tasted her the way he'd wanted to outside of the strict confines of their arrangement.

Slow.

There was no predetermined plan right now. No course of action that he had to follow. He could have her right here and now in the freshly planted garden, the last rays of sunlight caressing her sweet body. Or he could take her on the porch, with the motion of the swing pushing his body deeper into hers.

He could do anything. Everything.

He broke the kiss and rested his forehead against hers long enough to drag some air into his lungs and give his brain a much-needed burst of oxygen. As anxious as Josh was to be inside the hot, sweet woman in his arms, he'd waited too long for this to have it over so quickly. This wasn't about what he wanted. It was about what she wanted, and so he vowed to keep his head even if it killed him.

"Kiss me again," she said, as if she knew what drove his hesitancy.

He complied, but slower this time, more controlled. He let her take the lead. She plunged her tongue into his mouth and explored. He anchored his hands at her waist and held her close enough for her to feel the bulge in his jeans.

She trailed her hands over his chest, her fingers plucking at his T-shirt. She pressed her body up against him, rubbing herself up and down until he damn near exploded in his jeans. But then she pulled back enough for him to breathe.

She stared up at him. "Let's go inside."

He lifted her into his arms and carried her into the house and up the stairs. At the end of the hall, he stared down at her, his gaze questioning.

"Last door on the right."

He half expected another one of the dining rooms, but this was just a plain bedroom with a cedar double bed covered in a pale yellow comforter. Matching sheer curtains hung from the windows. Perfume and cosmetics lay spread across the matching cedar dresser. A Kiss the Cook apron hung from one corner of the dresser mirror.

He knew without asking that this was her room and a wave of satisfaction rolled through him. He pressed her down into the mattress and gave her a deep kiss before pulling away and standing beside the bed. He gripped his T-shirt and pulled it up and over his head.

She scrambled to her knees and reached out. She trailed her fingertips over the hard muscles of his chest and lower, over the ridges cutting his abdomen.

Josh stood stock-still beneath her probing, his body rigid, hurting for her in a way he'd never hurt for any woman.

When she moved to dip her hands beneath the waist of his jeans, he caught her wrists. "You do this to me." He pressed her fingers against the hard length beneath the zipper of his jeans. "*You.* It's not because we're role-playing or because the time is right and I'm in the mood. I just look at you and I want you. Any time. All the time." He urged one of her hands down between her own thighs and watched the desire flare in her eyes. "And I do this to you."

He could tell by the way her lips parted that she felt the heat through her pants, scorching her palm. Her lips parted on a gasp and her body trembled and it was all he could do not to lean down and kiss her again. And again.

Instead, he gathered his control and released her.

"It's your turn, cupcake." His muscles bunched with tension and restraint as he stared down at her, into her. "If you really want this, if you really want *me,* I need to know it."

And then, just as he'd promised himself out in the garden, he waited for Holly Farraday to make the next move.

12

HOLLY STARED UP at Josh, his gaze so dark and hot, and her body trembled in anticipation.

There were so many things she wanted to say.

I want you.

I need you.

I can't wait to touch you.

She opened her mouth, but the words seemed to stall on the tip of her tongue the way they always did.

But where she couldn't tell him, she could show him.

Holly sat back on her haunches and lifted her tank top over her head. Trembling fingers worked at the catch of her bra, freeing her straining breasts. She unbuttoned her shorts and sat back to work them down her legs. Her panties followed until she was completely naked.

He didn't reach out. He simply looked at her, yet it felt as if his hot hand traveled the length of her body along with his gaze, tweaking her nipples and circling the vee between her legs and stealing the air from her lungs.

Desire rushed through her, sharp and demanding, and she climbed to her knees and reached for him.

When she touched the waistband of his jeans this time, he didn't stop her. She slid the button free, her knuckles grazing his bare stomach. He drew in a sharp breath, but he didn't move. She slid the zipper down and the edges fell open. She hooked her fingers in the waistband of his briefs and tugged his jeans and underwear down just enough to free his massive erection. She touched the plump, ripe head with the tip of her finger and he groaned.

She trailed her fingers down his hardness, feeling his veins bulge and his shaft throb. She relished the feel of him for a few fast, furious heartbeats before he seemed to reach his limit.

With a throaty growl, he reached for her, pulling her close. He captured her mouth with his own and sucked the breath from her body with his hungry kiss. She met him thrust for thrust, lick for lick, losing herself in the storm of emotion that raged inside her body.

A moment later, he pressed her back against the bed, then leaned away.

"Holly."

At the sound of his voice, she opened her eyes and stared up into the stormy depths of his.

"Don't close your eyes. I want to see everything that you feel. I want to know that you like it when I touch you. That you want me to touch you. *Me.*" He settled beside her and trailed his hand down her collarbone, the slope of one breast. "Do you like it when I touch you here?" With his fingertip, he traced the outline of her nipple, circling the dark tip until it ripened.

"Yes," she murmured.

He smiled, then dipped his head to close his mouth

over one swollen tip. Holly gasped and wound her fingers in the silky roughness of his hair.

He sucked and nuzzled the throbbing nipple until Holly cried out. Then he kissed his way to the other and started to suckle.

Her nerves came alive as he moved his hands down to her waist. He leaned away from her then, letting the cool air blowing from the overhead air-conditioning vent breeze over her heated skin.

"You closed your eyes," he said.

Guilty, Holly lifted her heavy lids to stare up at him. Their gazes locked as he trailed his hand down her abdomen to the triangle of hair at the base of her thighs.

He watched her as he cupped the heated flesh between her legs. "You're so wet," he said, slipping one finger inside the soft folds.

Holly arched her back, pushing herself into his palm, drawing his touch deeper.

"You like me touching you like this?"

She nodded, staring up at him, her lips parted, her body alive with want.

"And like this?" He slipped another finger inside of her and Holly felt her body tighten around him. Need coiled in her stomach, winding tighter with each delicious stroke of his hand.

She took a ragged breath, then another and another as Josh played inside her, driving her toward a pleasure that was so fierce and intense she could hardly stand it.

She gasped, arching her hips for him. He pushed deeper, caressing and stroking until her legs trembled violently and her mind reeled from the sensations flooding her. Then he eased his hand away.

"Josh?" She forced her eyes open to find him studying her heated face.

"I'm here," he murmured. He took her wrist and pressed a lingering kiss to her pulse beat. "I know you want me, Holly. I can feel it. Can you feel it?" He closed his fingers over hers and touched her palm to her own cheek. She felt the fiery skin and her heart beat faster. He guided her hand from her cheek, down the column of her throat.

Her skin, so hot and flushed beneath her fingers, trembled from her own touch as Josh continued to guide her along. When she touched her nipple, the peak hardened even more. Desire, sharp and sweet, knifed through her. She started to pull away, frightened by the intensity of her reaction, but Josh held her steady.

"Don't stop," he said. "Feel how much you want me, Holly. Feel what I feel when I touch you." He drew her hand down across her stomach to the throbbing between her legs.

Her fingertips touched soft, dewy flesh and pleasure swamped her. She'd masturbated before, but this went beyond self-gratification. With him watching her, guiding her, the act took on a different meaning. It wasn't just about her own pleasure, but his, as well. She could see the heat in his gaze, the hunger as he guided her through each delicious stroke until she writhed and whimpered, desperate for release.

She cried out, feeling the gush of wetness against her own fingertips as release jolted through her. Josh held her hand steady, sending her higher than she'd ever gone before with the simple act.

"You're so beautiful," he whispered, his lips a steady vibration at her temple. He let go of her hand to feel his way up the length of her body.

She could feel him, hard and hot against her thigh, and she became aware of a renewed tightening inside. She watched as he reached down and pulled a foil packet from the pocket of his discarded jeans. Driven by her need for him, she took the condom from his hands and tore open the package. She eased the contents over the head of his smooth, pulsing shaft, feeling it twitch beneath her touch.

"Now it's my turn to feel you," she told him, relishing his deep, throaty groan as she slipped the second skin the rest of the way down. Then she turned to reach toward the opposite side of the bed and toss the empty package into the wastebasket.

He pressed his lips between her shoulder blades and her breath caught.

"How do I feel?" he murmured against her skin. He pressed his arousal between her buttocks and her mouth went dry.

"Like you really want me," she whispered, her heart pounding.

"Darlin', you don't know the half of it." He leaned up on his knees and pulled her up in front of him, his chest cradling her back. He swept her hair to the side and nibbled the side of her neck. One arm came around and he fingered her nipple, rolling and plucking until she gasped.

"I…" She swallowed and searched for her voice. "So show me."

He grabbed her by the hips and urged her forward until her bottom lifted toward him. The head of his erection slid along her damp flesh a split second before he drove into her. He filled her so completely, so perfectly, that Holly barely caught the cry that curled up her throat.

He gathered her close, one hand kneading her breast while the other moved down. His fingers slid over her fleshy mound and touched her tender flesh stretched tight over his erection.

"You hold me so well," he murmured against the curve of her throat. "So tight." The rough pad of his finger brushed her clitoris and a shiver ripped through her. Her body constricted around his and he groaned. He started to move then, in and out, the motion slow and steady at first as he rode her from behind.

She leaned forward, bracing her hands on the bed as she arched her back. The motion pushed her bottom back against him. She met him stroke for stroke until the ride picked up speed. They went faster. Higher. Until she couldn't hang on any longer. With a loud moan, she pushed back against him, drew him fully inside and let herself go. Light exploded behind her eyelids and convulsions gripped her body as she gave herself up to the delicious pleasure of wanting Josh McGraw.

JOSH THROBBED inside her, exploding with earthshaking intensity as her muscles clenched and unclenched around him. He slid his hands up her sweat-soaked back to weave his fingers into her damp hair and pull her back up against him. Burying his face in the fragrant crook of her neck, he held her close. He felt every quiver of her body, every erratic breath. Her heart pounded against the palm of his hand and his stomach hollowed out as if someone had sucker-punched him. A wave of possessiveness swept through him and he had the sudden, desperate urge to tighten his hold on her and never let go.

Because she was his.

He'd slept with numerous women, but none had ever stirred such a fierce response. Once Josh savored any particular woman, he usually lost his taste for her pretty quickly.

But not this woman. With each kiss, each touch, he wanted more.

For the moment.

Josh wasn't a man who put much weight in love or forever or any of that other bullshit men used to snag a woman and keep her with him through the lies and the betrayal. And so he wasn't placing any bets on the infatuation he felt for the woman in his arms, except to say that it would fade. It always faded.

And if it didn't?

He would still walk away.

The thought bothered him a lot more than it should have and he forced it aside, determined to focus on the here and now. On the steady beat of her heart and the sweet scent of her skin and the fact that they weren't bound by any agreement this time. He had all night to enjoy her and he intended to do just that.

"WHAT ARE YOU DOING?" Josh leaned up on his elbow and watched as Holly padded across the darkened bedroom and flipped on a small lamp.

"Getting dressed." She reached into her drawer and pulled on a large T-shirt that fell to midthigh.

"Why?"

"I thought I would walk you out." She turned and reached for his discarded jeans which she handed to him. "You'll need these. Though I suppose it wouldn't matter if you left in your skivvies. That's one plus of being out in the middle of nowhere."

"Let me get this straight," he said as he swung his legs over the side of the bed, the jeans in his hands, and stared at the clock. "You want me to leave?" It was just a little past one in the morning. "Now?"

She nodded. "I've got to be up early and I really need to get to bed."

He stared at her, his gaze traveling up her bare legs, over the soft white cotton, to her passion-swollen lips and bright green eyes. Her hair was mussed and she looked like a woman who'd just been made love to by her man. He patted the spot next to him and grinned. "So get back in bed."

Her lips curved into a knowing smile. "If I crawl back in that bed, we're not going to get any sleep. I've got one hundred and thirty orders to fill tomorrow."

"You really want me to *leave?*"

"I need some sleep."

"So do I; but I was thinking we could do that right here. Together." With his body wrapped around hers.

"I can't actually sleep with someone else in the bed.

Even when I was little, I never slept over at anyone's house. Whenever I tried, I ended up staring at the ceiling all night because I just couldn't get comfortable."

"Because it didn't feel like home," he told her. "Did it?"

She gave him a sharp look before she finally shrugged. "I never could really relax no matter how much I tried. Needless to say, I wasn't at the top of anyone's list when it came to slumber party invites."

"I don't know about that. You'd be top on my list."

She gave him a knowing look. "Your slumber party wouldn't involve Barbies and popcorn."

"I don't know about the popcorn, but you've definitely outgrown the Barbies. You like bigger dolls now, and so do I." Her cheeks fired a bright red at the reminder of their threesome encounter not long ago, and he felt a swell of satisfaction.

For all her boldness, he could still make her blush.

Even more, he liked making her blush. He liked seeing her all soft and vulnerable. Even more, he liked the sudden surge of possessiveness it inspired.

As fast as the feeling stirred, he tamped it back down, because Josh had been doing it so long he wasn't so sure he could ever stop.

Even if he suddenly wanted to.

"I've got an early day tomorrow, and I'm sure you do, too." She snatched up his T-shirt and handed it to him. "It's best if we call it a night."

He opened his mouth to argue, but there was something almost desperate about the way she looked at him. As if she needed him to leave right now, as much as she'd needed him to stay earlier.

"I do have to finish the branding on the new cattle."

"See? We've both got a full schedule. Speaking of which, I need to make sure I made the list of ingredients for tomorrow's orders. We're still running a day behind because Duke keeps delivering late, so I try to inventory everything beforehand to make sure I'm stocked. Otherwise, we're running to the Food-o-rama or picking up extra supplies when I go to Cherryville, which wastes so much time. You can show yourself out, can't you?" Before he could reply, she pressed a kiss to his lips and walked out.

What the hell just happened?

The question echoed in his head as he sat on the edge of the bed and listened to her soft footsteps until they'd disappeared downstairs. He eyed the indentation on the mattress where they'd lain together only a short time ago. He barely resisted the urge to crawl between the sweet-smelling sheets—sheets that smelled of her—and give in to the exhaustion tugging at his muscles. At the same time, he couldn't forget the desperation in her gaze.

"Shit," he muttered as he tugged on his clothes. A few minutes later, he stepped down off her front porch, his boots crunching gravel as he headed for his pickup truck.

So much for enjoying her all night.

JOSH FLICKED a button on the work light and watched as bright rays flooded the old barn and pushed back the shadows. He popped the hood on the old GTO, hooked a small, portable light overhead and started unscrewing the cracked transmission.

The twisted metal refused to give and he reached for a hammer. He positioned his screwdriver and hammered the flat head into the groove. He pried and jimmied and worked at the engine for the next half hour, determined to get the damned thing out one way or another, and his mind completely off Holly and the fact that she'd kicked him out of bed.

It didn't matter.

It shouldn't matter.

Hell, he never spent the night with a woman unless they were going at it. But just to sleep? He usually walked away even faster than Holly had. So why did it bother him so much?

Because she'd been the one walking away and he couldn't help but wonder...why?

The question had nagged him all the way home and into bed where he'd tossed and turned before finally giving up. He'd needed a distraction and so he'd come out here to work. To forget.

He jammed the screwdriver deeper and pried until he heard metal crack. The transmission gave with a loud creak and a groan and he pulled it free. Christ, it was a mess. His dad had not only done himself in when he'd hit the pole. He'd annihilated the car, as well.

The thought didn't stir the same bitterness that it usually did and Josh couldn't help but remember Holly's words.

Maybe it wasn't guilt so much as grief.

Had his father really loved his mother even though he'd lied and cheated? He wasn't so sure anymore. Not that it mattered. They'd both died miserable and hurt.

At the same time, the possibility that his father had been capable of such an emotion, that he'd felt it so deeply he hadn't wanted to live without his wife, meant that such a feeling existed. And that it was powerful. And that maybe, just maybe, Josh could feel the same thing someday.

Of course, he would handle things differently, that was for damned sure. He wouldn't cheat and he wouldn't lie and he wouldn't add to his past mistakes.

If...

The possibility weighed on his mind as he worked at the transmission and tried to forget Holly and the way she'd shoved him out of bed.

He'd obviously smelled too many exhaust fumes. It wasn't about sleeping with her. It was about everything before they got around to sleeping. He'd wanted to violate the agreement, and he'd done just that. They were free. That was all that mattered. That they could do what they wanted, when they wanted, period.

Not *sleeping* with her, for chrissake. Sleeping meant a real relationship. Hell, it was one step away from a ring and a lifetime of servitude.

At least that's what Josh told himself over the next few weeks as he and Holly not only finished the menu selections, with the exception of the elusive house special, but came up with a few delicacies of their own. The trouble was, the more time he spent with her, the more he started to think that it might be nice, real nice, to not only hold her in his arms all night, but wake up next to her in the morning.

Every morning.

His brain must be fogged. That was the only explanation. Because no way was Josh falling for one particular woman. No damn way.

"No LACTOSE or strawberries," Holly told old Duke early the next morning on the way back from the library. After two hours searching old newspapers for some clue as to the house special, she'd given up.

But not on Duke. Not without giving it one more try.

The old man eyed the platter of Climactic Cookies and shook his head. "My boy cain't do oats. Gets all red and itchy and his throat damn near closes up. *Everybody* knows that."

Everybody but Holly.

"Then again," he continued, "I'm sure it was an honest mistake. You wouldn't be privy to that information being from Huntsville and all."

"It's Houston."

"Houston?" He shook his head. "Never did like those Oilers back in the day 'afore they lost their common sense and hightailed it to Tennessee. The Cowboys… now there's a football team worth its salt." He glanced behind him. "Speaking of which, ESPN's about to show highlights from the last game." He took the platter of cookies from her hands. "You just run on along now and I'll take care of these."

Strike three…you're outttt!

"Do YOU EVER SLEEP?"

At the sound of Sue's voice, Holly glanced up from the stack of pictures in her hand. She sat cross-legged on the floor surrounded by stacks of pictures, old magazines and past issues of the *Romeo Daily*. She'd already sorted through everything, but now it was time to get organized and get everything packed away into boxes for storage.

"It's nearly noon."

"Too early for a woman who's been burning the candle till all hours."

"I didn't work late last night."

"I'm talking personally. Grace Jackson at the dry cleaner's heard from her son who works at the gas station who heard from Mr. Milby who drives the feed delivery truck that a certain pickup truck was still parked in your driveway as of midnight last night."

"Mr. Milby was delivering feed at midnight?"

"Actually, he was hog hunting up the road at Marv Jackson's place—it's better at night—and he saw Josh's truck on his way over." Her eyes lit. "He spent the night, didn't he?"

"He did not spend the night."

"But he *was* here after hours," Sue prodded, obviously wanting more details.

But Holly had never been into details. She'd never been the center of attention in the girls' locker room. Never dished about her dates or confided a crush. She'd been too busy keeping her distance, mentally preparing herself for the next move. And the next. And the next.

Not this time, she reminded herself.

"If you tell me he was cutting the grass, I'm going to crawl into that supersize commercial oven of yours and turn it on high," Sue pressed. "Come on. Be a good friend and throw me a bone. Let me live vicariously through you."

Holly gave in to the smile tugging at her lips. "He wasn't cutting the grass."

"I didn't think so."

"We've been seeing each other." When Sue's smile faded, Holly rushed on, "Since you let him down easy, that is."

"I tried to be as nice as I could. I mean, he's so good-looking, but he's just not Bert Wayne. Speaking of which—" she took Holly's hands "—it happened."

"Bert Wayne asked you back?"

"Not officially. But he called this morning and said he wants to talk. He's coming by my place tonight for dinner." Excitement lit her eyes. "This is it, Holly. He's going to take me back. I just know it."

"That's great."

"That's why I came by so early. I've got a million things to do today—I scheduled a facial and a mud bath over at Earline's in half an hour—but I wanted to tell you the good news and say thank you. If I hadn't met you at the saloon that night, I don't think I would have had the courage to do any of this." She held up her hands and indicated the Daisy Duke short-shorts she wore, complete with a red-and-white checkered peasant blouse that rode low on her shoulders and matching high heels. "There you were about to change your life by moving to a small town where you had no friends whatsoever, while I was doing nothing but wallowing in my own misery. Why, it was positively life-changing, that's what it was. Talk about courageous. You had nobody, meanwhile I was surrounded by friends and still couldn't pull myself together enough to make a change."

"Um, thanks."

"Not only didn't you have friends, but didn't have a clue as to how to take care of a place this size."

"I was a little overwhelmed."

"Most people would have given up after the first tractor incident, but not you. You've got guts."

That, or a great big hole in her head.

"I couldn't very well keep feeling sorry for myself when you had all the odds against you—heck, you still do—but you're still trying anyway."

"Thanks. I, um, think."

Sue smiled. "You deserve some fun with Josh. Speaking of which, if I'm going to show Bert Wayne just how fun I can be, I need to get going. After Earline's, I've got an appointment at the Hair Saloon for my hair and nails. And then I've got to practice in case things get really hot and heated once he asks to come home."

Practice?

Holly had a quick mental image of Sue and Billy the Buckaroo—the *Warm Bodies* doll—before she managed to force it away.

Some things were better left alone.

"I'll see you Monday." She gave Holly a quick hug, knocking over a stack of pictures in the process. "Look at me! I'm so excited I'm a nervous wreck." She reached for the scattered photographs. "Your grandmother really was a beautiful woman," she said as she picked up one black-and-white photo in particular.

Red Rose Farraday stood on the front porch surrounded by her "girls." It was the actual picture that had inspired the portrait that sat in Holly's bedroom. The same artistic rendition that graced the front of the infamous menu.

"Back then," Holly said, remembering the more recent photographs she'd found of her grandmother just before she'd passed away. "But her lifestyle caught up with her and took its toll."

"I don't think it was her lifestyle, so much as it was Mother Nature. Everybody gets old. But some give up along with it. They let their spirits die long before anything else. I think that's what happened with your grandmother. For whatever reason, she gave up. But not everybody goes quietly. Take Miss Martha, there." She pointed to the woman on the far right. "She's every bit as spunky as she always was and it keeps her looking and acting young. At the rate she's going, she'll probably live to be a hundred, and not look a day over seventy-five."

"Miss Martha?" Holly eyed the slender young woman and for the first time, she noted the china cup and saucer she held in her hand. A smile curved her lips. A familiar smile. "But that's Hearty Marty." Her heart kicked up speed as the truth registered.

"Marty, as in Martha," Sue said. "Miss Martha. The lady who owns the tearoom."

13

"YOU USED TO work for my grandmother," Holly said that afternoon when she walked into Miss Martha's Tearoom to find the old woman arranging a plate of petit fours.

"Keep it down, child," the old woman said, motioning to the table of women that sat in the far corner, sampling pimento cheese and watercress sandwiches. "I've got customers."

"You're Hearty Marty." Holly slid into the seat across from Miss Martha.

"Once upon a time, but thanks to high blood pressure and my diabetes, I get shaky when the wind blows. I ain't nearly the healthy horse I once was." A wistful smile touched the old woman's lips. "I'm afraid those days are gone forever." She finished the petit fours and placed them in the glass display case before reaching for another platter and a box of tea biscuits.

"Why didn't you tell me?"

"You didn't ask. Besides, that isn't the sort of thing I go around telling folks."

"I'm sorry. Of course not. It's probably better forgotten."

"Are you kidding? That was the happiest, most exciting time of life, which is precisely the reason I keep my mouth shut. Why, if those busybody Juliets were to find out I was one of Rose's girls, I wouldn't get a moment's peace. They'd be after me to find out all of my secrets what with them all so obsessed with pleasing their men. They ought to start with some blessed silence. I swear I ain't met a one of 'em—and I've met 'em all since they're in and out of here lunching all the time—that can keep quiet for two minutes. And I surely ain't ever met a man who likes to listen to all that nonsense all the time."

It was the happiest, most exciting time of my life....

The words echoed in Holly's head and she remembered the pictures of her mother. She'd never realized her mother could actually smile so much. She hadn't looked at all like a woman who'd been stuck in a bad situation. She'd looked...happy.

"She was happy," Miss Martha said as if reading Holly's mind.

"I beg your pardon?"

"Your mother. That's why you're here, isn't it? Because you want to know about her. I knew the first time I met you that you had it all wrong. You talked about her as if she had every right to run away."

"She was in a bad situation. I would have—"

"You would have stayed," Miss Martha cut in. "You would have stayed because your mother loved you and wanted the best for you and you would have respected her for it. But your mother resented Rose."

"What are you talking about?"

"Your mother was too much like Rose. Pessimistic

when it came to men and relationships. Distrustful. Jaded." Her gaze met Holly's. "She never fantasized about getting married or having kids or living happily ever after like other young girls her age. She didn't have any big dreams beyond joining the other girls at the Farraday Inn, and it broke Rose's heart. She'd started her business out of necessity. She'd wanted to provide for your mother and give her the choices she'd never had. Instead, she inadvertently taught your mother that a body was just another thing to be bartered or sold. She hated herself for that and she was determined to save your mother and give her a chance at a normal life. She made arrangements to send her to live with her second cousin in Arizona. Your mother didn't want to go and so she ran away."

The full weight of the truth weighed down on Holly and she sank to the edge of the sofa. Memories rushed at her and tears burned her eyes. They'd run so many times, picking up at the spur of the moment and moving on to escape her mother's past. To outrun her legacy.

Or so Holly had thought when she'd discovered her grandmother's identity. "I thought she left home because she didn't want to end up like her mother." Her memory reached back to the child's drawings she'd found along with the pictures. There'd been so many of them. So much love. "She wanted to be just like her, didn't she?"

Miss Martha nodded. "Rose loved Jeanine too much to let that happen. She'd convinced herself that she could keep things strictly business and keep our way of life from tainting Jeanine. She never let the girls walk around with little on, and she sure as heck didn't let any customers in the house while Jeanine was there." At Holly's raised eyebrow, Miss Martha added, "Rose and Jeanine lived in a small cottage that used to be out back. I know it was crazy for her to think that Jeanine could be so close and not realize what was going on, but we all put on blinders every now and then. Rose thought Jeanine believed the inn to be a restaurant like everybody else. Until one Saturday afternoon when Jeanine showed up wearing one of Rose's old negligees. She was fourteen and it was career week at school."

"And she'd made her career choice," Holly added.

"Exactly." Miss Martha smiled, as if remembering. "I'd never seen Rose so shocked in all my life. And angry. Why, she marched Jeanine back to the cottage and grounded her for two weeks. That's when Rose finally admitted to herself that Jeanine knew and, even worse, she approved of Rose's business. She admired it. She aspired to step up and take Rose's place when the time came. Rose vowed she would never let that happen and so she wrote to her second cousin and made the arrangements for Jeanine to go to this fancy girls' school in Arizona. She was determined to give Jeanine a better way of life." Miss Martha shook her head. "But the girl had her own ideas and so she packed up and left. Rose was devastated. She closed up the inn and cried for weeks, until she smartened up and realized that she needed the money from the inn if she hoped to find Jeanine. She hired several private investigators and she came close to catching up with your mother many times."

Holly's mind raced and she thought back to her child-hood, to the first memory she had of her mother pack-ing them up. "But my mom stayed one step ahead and kept us moving."

Miss Martha nodded. "When Rose finally caught up to Jeanine in Chicago, it was too late. Your mother had just died. Rose tore down the cottage then and gave up hope of Jeanine ever coming back. By the time she found out about you, you'd gone into the system. She knew she didn't stand a chance in hell of getting cus-tody of you, not with her background, so she stayed away. She had no choice." The old woman touched Holly's cheek. "But she was always there, keeping an eye on you. Helping out when you needed her."

Holly thought of the large grant that had miracu-lously appeared after every bank in town, and on the In-ternet, had turned her down when she'd been trying to launch Sweet & Sinful.

"She's the one who helped me start my business, wasn't she? She was the source of the grant."

Martha gave her a knowing smile. "She was mighty proud when you graduated from college. It was her gift to you."

"I wish I had known."

"She wanted you to. At the same time, she was afraid of what you would think of her. Jeanine left here as mad as a hornet because Rose wanted to send her away. She didn't know if Jeanine ever got over that hurt and real-ized it was for her own good, or if it turned into hate and she passed it on to you."

But the only thing Jeanine Farraday had passed on

was her fear of getting close to anyone. In her eyes, she'd been betrayed by Rose who'd wanted to send her away, and so she'd raised her own daughter to keep her emotions to herself. To stay distant and guarded and wary when it came to people. To trust no one.

No trust, no bust.

The notion echoed in Holly's head and caused a tightness in her chest. She blinked back a sudden rush of tears.

"What was my grandmother really like?"

"She was beautiful, but you already know that. What most folks don't realize is that she was smart, too. And she had a big heart. She looked out for her girls and she didn't put up with nonsense. Why, I remember the time when old Wilbur—he was this rancher from Blue County—came out to our place and tried to give Rose an IOU for my company. That didn't sit too well, I can tell you right now. She pulled out her old shotgun and put him to work in the laundry room until he'd washed and folded every last sheet and towel. And then she handed him over to me. Let me tell you, I put that man to work washing my unmentionables, until his hands pruned up and he practically begged for mercy. Of course, I showed him a little once I felt he'd learned his lesson. I was sweet on him for a while and I never could resist a man with his shirtsleeves rolled up and a wet pair of undies in his hands. Not to mention, he brought me a big bouquet of flowers on his next visit. And his next. And eventually an engagement ring. Not that I married him, mind you. He just wasn't my type. But then there was Jessie Langford. Tall, dark and handsome, and he knew how to treat a lady. Never showed up without a great big box of candy in his hands. And he did this thing when he kissed." The old woman gave an excited shiver. "I've never been one to kiss and tell, so let's just say that man was sweeter than a box of Hershey's chocolate and just as sinful…."

While Miss Martha went on about her past loves, Holly's own past kept nagging at her.

No trust, no bust.

Holly had learned well. Too well. Despite her own vow to settle down and start cultivating relationships, she was still running from the people in her life, still putting up walls, still terrified of getting hurt.

Still sleeping alone.

Because of Josh. She was holding back because it was pointless to fall in love with a man who didn't believe in the concept.

At least that's what she'd been telling herself.

But it was just an excuse to keep from taking a chance and getting hurt. While she couldn't make Josh return her feelings, she could be true to herself. Honest. Open. Regardless of the consequences.

Better to have loved and lost…

She'd always thought the saying completely ludicrous. But as she listened to Miss Martha reminisce about her past and saw the happiness in the old woman's eyes, Holly realized that she, herself, wanted to feel the same way. Just once.

"Miss Martha," Holly said when the woman finished her stories and Holly pushed to her feet to leave. "I know you've never been one to kiss and tell, but there's one thing that's been driving me crazy."

"Yes, child?"

"What *was* the house special?"

"SORRY, I'M LATE," Josh said when Holly opened the door to him on Friday afternoon. "I got stuck with a feed delivery at the last minute, but if we hurry, we'll just make the chamber of commerce meeting—" His words stumbled to a halt as Holly stepped into full view.

She wore a faint smile and nothing else, and the sight stalled the air in his chest.

A damned crazy reaction considering the fact that he'd seen her naked more times than he could count. But damned if it didn't feel like the first time all over again. He swept a gaze from her head to her pink-tipped toes, pausing at all the mouthwatering spots in between, like a hungry man eyeing his next meal.

The sun's last rays caressed her body and made her skin glow. She wasn't a thin woman by far, but her weight was proportioned in all the right places, giving her delicious curves that made his hands itch for a touch. Dark, ripe, red nipples tipped her full pink breasts. Her small waist flared into full, rounded hips and a shapely ass. A narrow strip of blond hair covered her fleshy mound and disappeared between her long legs. Trim ankles led to small, shapely feet.

"I..." He licked his lips and forced his gaze back up. The hunger that gleamed in her eyes hit him even harder than the sight of her naked body and need tightened his gut and twisted it into a knot. "I, um, thought we were going to the—" The words stalled as she took a deep breath, her breasts heaving and her nipples reaching out to him, and he forgot what he'd been about to say. "What is this?" he finally managed to utter after several frantic heartbeats.

Her smiled widened. "This is the house special." And then she pulled him inside, reached for the edge of his T-shirt and began to strip him down right there in the foyer. He wanted to ask for some specifics, but things were getting too hot, too fast. She peeled his clothes away with an urgency that was contagious, and so Josh followed her lead. He pushed her up against the wall and thrust deep inside.

Josh went completely still as he buried himself deep inside her hot, tight heat. He'd expected it to be good—it was always good. But he wasn't prepared for the sudden rush of feeling, so strong and overpowering, that went through him and threatened to knock him on his ass.

He braced himself against the piercing, sweet sensation, every muscle in his body locked tight.

His gaze caught and held hers and she didn't close her eyes the way she had their first time together when he'd been on top. She looked back at him, into him and he saw everything he felt mirrored deep in her eyes. Something passed between them, like a rope slipping around his body, winding tight and pulling him closer, until they were fused, connected.

One. It was a crazy notion. Sappy and sentimental and romantic and plumb *loco*.

Even so, it was there. Intense. Unexpected. *Real*.

She leaned forward and licked his pulse beat and he couldn't help himself, he slid his arms around her and simply held her for the next few moments. His heart beat against hers and their breaths mingled. His dick throbbed inside her and her insides tightened, flexing around him, holding him tight.

One.

Before he could dwell on the notion, she shimmied, drawing him deeper. A rush of pleasure pierced his brain and he forgot everything going on in his head and focused on his body and the need gripping him so tight he could hardly breathe.

He started to move, plunging into her with a fierce rhythm. He dipped his head and caught her nipple, sucking it into the wet heat of his mouth and feasting on her like a man possessed. He moved faster and harder, and sucked longer and deeper, until she thrashed wildly in his arms.

He released her breast and caught the exquisite cry that burst from her lips. Her muscles clamped around him, milking him greedily as her climax vibrated through her body. The sensation pulled him in for another fierce thrust and held him rigid as he exploded inside her.

He wasn't sure how he made it to her bedroom. He just knew that one moment he was resting his forehead against hers, his hands kneading her luscious bottom, and the next he was easing her onto the bed and following her down.

He spooned her, pulling her up tight against his body. He smoothed his hand over her hair and kissed her temple, and tried to come to terms with what had just happened.

Sex, his brain screamed. But it felt like something

altogether different. And when he heard the steady sound of Holly's breathing and realized that she'd fallen asleep, he knew beyond a doubt.

He wanted to think about what the realization meant, but he couldn't seem to keep his own eyes open. He closed them and gave in to the exhaustion tugging at his senses. He'd think about it tomorrow and then he'd figure out what the hell he was going to do because no way could he walk away from her.

At the same time, he couldn't not walk away. Holly wanted the big *L*. The real thing. She deserved it. She deserved a man who could love her back totally, completely, beyond a doubt. And as much as Josh felt for her, he just didn't know if it was enough.

"IT'S ABOUT TIME you answered your phone." Mason's voice carried over Josh's cell phone when he pressed the talk button.

"What time is it?"

"Time to rise and shine. It's six in the morning, bro. You should be on your second cup of coffee by now."

Josh blinked and adjusted his eyes to the dimly lit bedroom and the woman snuggled up against him. A faint breeze blew through the open window, stirring the curtains and sending a shiver up his arm. The heat wave was lifting just a little, although the days were still hot. But the nights had started to cool down and the sun had yet to rise.

"Josh?" Mason's voice drew him back to the present.

"Hold on a sec," he said. He eased his arm from beneath Holly's head. She stirred a moment before snuggling down into the pillow. Josh pulled the blanket up over her naked body and tucked the edge around her bare shoulder before turning to pull on his jeans. A few minutes later, he walked out onto the front porch and sat down on the porch steps.

"Hello?" Mason's voice slid into his ear.

"Yeah, I'm here."

"It's about damned time. I'm in a hurry."

"Another dinner date?"

"It's not even sunup. Besides, I haven't had a dinner date since I went all out and put the moves on the teacher. I figured I'd come on strong and scare her into submission like you suggested."

"And she slapped you and ordered you out of her house?"

"She practically tied me to the bedposts. It's a wonder I got away with my virtue still intact. I've been in hiding ever since. But thankfully, I'm home free now."

"You're finished?"

"And how."

"When do I get to see you?"

"If you hop in your truck and get your sorry ass home, I'd say in about fifteen minutes."

HOLLY WATCHED from the kitchen window as Josh's truck disappeared down the road before turning her attention to the note he'd left her.

Last night was incredible.

                                        Josh

He'd tried to wake her, but she'd pretended to be asleep. She hadn't wanted to face him. She couldn't. She closed her eyes and tried to swallow the sudden lump in her throat.

"You're home?"

She could still hear Josh's voice through the open bedroom window from the front porch below. While Josh hadn't mentioned a name, she'd known who it was and the truth had jerked her back to reality.

They'd sampled the last and final menu selection last night and his brother had come home. Their relationship was now officially over. She'd accumulated enough research to make the recipes more than credible. Josh had fulfilled his obligations to his family. It was over.

Despite last night.

She could easily understand why the uncomplicated, no-nonsense-style sex had been her grandmother's most popular offering. There'd been something so intense about it, so different, so *special*. Staring into his eyes— the key ingredient in the recipe—she'd felt connected to him in a way she'd never felt with any man before. It had only been a few hours and already she wanted to feel the sensation again.

She wanted to feel him.

Tears burned her eyes and she reached for her notebook. She needed to distance herself from what they'd shared. But writing down the details didn't help her gain any perspective this time. Things were different now. She was different.

She was in love.

But Josh McGraw didn't love her back.

Last night was incredible.

That's all he'd written. No *I love you. I can't live without you. Come away with me....*

She nixed the last thought. He would never ask her such a thing because he knew she would never do it. She couldn't. She'd been moving her entire life and she'd finally settled down.

And settled in.

A truth that should have hit home a half hour later when she heard a knock on the front door.

"You win," Delivery Duke declared when Holly found him standing on her doorstep. "Now just stop it, wouldya?"

Her gaze shifted to the stack of boxes beside him and relief rushed through her. "Is that my late delivery?"

"Actually, it's today's delivery. I sort of misplaced the late one. But I'll find it and get it out to you as soon as possible. Just promise you'll stay away from my dad."

"What are you talking about?"

"He's a diabetic and his sugar has been three times the normal amount since you and your desserts moved to town." He frowned. "I know what you're up to. You think if you get him all worked up in a sugar frenzy, that I'll be too worried to make my deliveries and somebody else will take my place. But it ain't gonna happen 'cause I got your number. I know all about you city people. All hustle and bustle. You never take time to smell the coffee in life and you think everybody else ought to rush around just like you. Why, it's people like you that suck the life right out of folks like me."

"Actually, the desserts were for you. I was trying to be neighborly."

He looked startled for a second before he seemed to dismiss the notion. "That's the craziest thing I ever heard. Why, I can't do dairy or strawberries or oats. Everybody—"

"—knows that," she finished. "I know. Your dad told me. He also said he was going to feed the desserts to his hogs. I had no idea he was diabetic, or that he was eating what I dropped off."

He gave her a do-I-look-like-I-just-fell-off-the-turnip-truck look.

Ahem. No comment.

"Look, just keep your fancy desserts away from my dad and I'll make sure I get out here every day with your deliveries."

"First thing in the morning?" When he shook his head, she added, "I've got a Warm Fudge Foreplay and I know how to use it."

"All right, all right."

Score one for Holly.

No more late deliveries. No more bending over backward to fit in. No more feeling like an outsider.

She was home. Really and truly *home*.

But as she went about her day, the old farmhouse didn't seem nearly as warm and welcoming as it had the day she'd first arrived. Rather, it felt cold. Lonely. *Empty*.

The way she now felt inside.

Holly had known it would be hard to say goodbye to

Josh, she just hadn't realized how hard until she'd fallen asleep in his arms.

Until she'd awoken without him and realized that she would do so for the rest of her life.

14

THEY NEEDED TO TALK.

The truth echoed in Josh's head as he drove the dirt road leading to the Farraday Inn. It had been a week since she'd met him at the doorway for their last recipe and his brother had rolled back into town. Seven days since she'd pretended to be asleep to avoid having to talk to him.

She'd thought she'd fooled him, but he'd known by the shallowness of her breathing that she'd been awake. And afraid. And so he hadn't pushed her for answers then.

Hell, he hadn't had an answer of his own. He'd needed to think. To understand what it was that had him tied up in knots.

He'd spent the time since then catching up on old times with his brother, finishing up the restoration of the GTO and trying to get a grip on the strange feelings that rolled around in his gut and kept him thinking that maybe, just maybe, he wasn't half as excited about the prospect of leaving as he was about staying.

Staying, for chrissake. He still couldn't believe he was even considering such a thing. But he was. He would. If she felt even a fourth of what he felt for her—

love or lust or a combination of the two. He wasn't sure since he'd never felt anything like it. He just knew it was strong and he needed to know if she felt the same.

He needed her to admit it to him.

If not…

He shook away the notion and turned into her driveway. He'd given her some time to think, to see if she missed him the way he'd missed her, but he'd had enough. He was through worrying and wondering. It was time to come clean. One way or another.

As he stepped up on the porch, a strange prickle worked its way up his spine. Something was wrong. He knew it even before he knocked on the door and no one answered.

He tried the knob. It turned easily in his hand and a few moments later he found himself standing in her kitchen.

An empty kitchen.

No countertops cluttered with flour and sugar. No mixers. No measuring cups. No bakery boxes.

Dread churned in his gut as he walked from room to room. The original furniture was still there, but the extra touches that had made the house Holly's were gone. There were no vases here and there, no freshly picked flowers, no cooking school certificate hanging on the wall, no *Home Sweet Home* quilt draped over the sofa—

The last thought stopped him cold and turned the dread to full-blown panic as the truth hit him.

She was gone.

Fear hit him then like a two-by-four smacking upside his head. Every bone in his body went rigid. His muscles tightened. His heart pounded. The air rushed from his chest. His stomach bottomed out. Josh nearly doubled over from the pain of it all and he knew then that this was the feeling he would face every day for the rest of his life if he walked away from Romeo.

This…emptiness.

The truth crystallized in his brain, his heart as he stood in the cold, lifeless kitchen. What he felt was real, all right. So real it hurt to breathe. His chest hitched as he tried to draw some air into his lungs. Anxiety washed through him and he turned, forcing his legs to move. He walked back out, climbed into his truck. The tires kicked up dirt and gravel as he turned the vehicle around and peeled out of her driveway and headed for town.

There was no way he was letting her go now, whether she admitted her feelings or not. If he had to, he would wait for her and give her as much time as she needed to come to her senses.

And if she didn't?

Well, he still wasn't going anywhere. He *loved* her, dammit. Josh McGraw, a man who didn't believe in love, was stuck smack-dab in the middle of the emotion. Lost in it. Driven by it.

He had to tell her.

But first, Josh McGraw had to find her.

"WHERE IS SHE?" he demanded as he burst into Mike Davidson's office a frantic twenty minutes later.

The attorney glanced up from the stack of documents in front of him and frowned at the intrusion. Old Mr. Perkins sat on the opposite side of the desk, a startled look on his face.

"Good God, boy, you scared the bejesus out of me,

and right before I signed my Last Will and Testament. What in tarnation is wrong with you?"

"I have to know where she went," he told Mike. "You know, don't you?"

The lawyer frowned a moment more before he finally shrugged. "Give me a minute." He handed Mr. Perkins the documents in his hand and a pen and left him signing the papers while he ushered Josh into the outer office. "She doesn't want to see you."

"She's still here?" Hope blossomed in Josh's chest and his heart pounded faster. "She didn't leave?"

"She found a little place in town. Moved in yesterday. I guess living out at Rose's place wasn't what she'd hoped." He walked over to a file cabinet and pulled a set of blue bound papers from inside. "She asked me to give you this."

Josh stared at the deed to the land. Not the agreed upon twenty-five acres, but all fifty. And the house.

"It's back in McGraw hands again, the deed free and clear, just like your granddaddy always wanted."

Just like Josh had wanted for the past six months. This was the last of it. The final act to right his grandfather's wrongs and, in the process, ease Josh's own guilt over lying to his mother.

He hadn't wanted to believe that he'd been trying to exorcise his own demons, but he knew now that Holly had been right. It hadn't been about making up for his grandfather's mistakes. It had been about trying to fix his own. Or at least live with himself a little easier.

But Josh had already forgiven himself. He'd done

that the night he'd opened up to Holly, talked about his past and admitted his mistake.

You were just a kid.

She'd been so understanding, so forgiving and so right. He'd been young, naive, stupid. But he hadn't meant to hurt anyone. He knew that now and he felt, deep inside, that somehow his mother knew it, too. And that she understood.

"I thought you were crazy offering all that money for twenty-five acres. But for the whole spread, it makes a lot more sense. I'll need you to sign a few papers for the purchase," Mike started, but Josh cut him off.

"Later. I've got something I have to take care of. Tell me where she is." He turned expectant eyes on Mike. The attorney gave him a stubborn look before he finally shrugged.

"I'll have you know that this violates the confidentiality clause in my contract." He scribbled an address on a slip of paper and handed it to Josh. "I hope for the both of us that you know what you're doing."

"So do I," he said as he took the paper. "So do I."

"YOU FINISH UP with a dollop of sweet whipping cream," Holly said as she held up the gourmet dessert, "and bingo, you've got yourself an Ultimate Orgasm. Slice and serve, and your man will melt. Guaranteed. Of course, wearing nothing but an apron and your best smile is sure to speed up the process."

The expected round of applause erupted as she handed the dessert to the woman on her right to be passed around, and gathered up her notes.

"That wasn't exactly what we expected." Lolly Langtree met her as she stepped down off the podium. "It was a cooking lesson," she said accusingly.

"You wanted an Ultimate Orgasm and they're my specialty."

"But—"

"I thought it was great. I can't wait to make it for Melvin." Another woman that Holly recognized from the initial Juliet welcoming wagon stepped up to her. "Why, he loves to eat and I'm sure he'll be so grateful, he'll do any and everything I ask. Do you have any extra copies of the recipe? I'd like to send one to my sister up in Austin. She loves to bake."

"Of course." Holly handed her a copy.

"Me, too," another woman said, reaching out.

"And me."

Much to her surprise, Holly spent the next fifteen minutes handing out copies of her coveted recipe and giving cooking tips to a crowd of eager Juliets.

"What happened to the menu of sexual delights?" The deep, husky voice slid into her ears as she walked out of the dining room, her briefcase in hand, and stopped her just shy of the front door.

"I…" she started as she turned to find Josh leaning just outside the dining room archway, his arms folded, a strange look in his eyes.

Outside, branches swayed with a slight afternoon breeze. Rays of sunshine filtered through the front windows of the restaurant and chased shadows across his heavily stubbled face.

He looked as bad as she felt. She noted the tight lines

around his mouth, the shadows beneath his eyes, as if he hadn't slept any more than she had the past week, as if he'd done his own tossing and turning. As if he'd been as lonely and upset.

As if.

Her heart pounded. A strange sensation to a woman who'd felt nothing but a slow, dull, aching thud in her chest for the past several days.

She swallowed against the sudden tightness in her throat. "What are you doing here?" she finally managed.

"I asked first. What about all the research we did? What was the purpose of all that touching and kissing and loving?"

The questions stirred a rush of images and her body trembled. "I guess I'm not one to kiss and tell." When he continued to stare at her, into her, she shrugged. "It didn't feel right talking about it. About us."

"Is that why you moved out of the house? Because it didn't feel right?"

She wanted to tell him to mind his own business. To take the house and the land, no questions asked. But there was a sincerity in his gaze, as if he really and truly cared about her answer. "Too many memories."

"I thought you wanted memories."

"I do, that's why I moved out. I need to start over and make my own memories." *Without you.* She didn't say the words, but she didn't have to. He knew. "I want a real home of my own making. A place where I belong."

"That's fine with me so long as there's plenty of room in the bathroom. I know how you women can be with all that perfume and makeup. I need at least a place to stash my shaving cream and razor."

"Your shaving cream..." Her words trailed off as she tried to absorb what he was saying. He couldn't... He wouldn't...

She noted the strange twinkle in his eyes, the flash of desperation, and her mind snagged on something he'd said earlier.

What was the purpose of all that touching and kissing and loving?

Loving. As in *love.*

"What are you doing here?" she asked again. The answer was there, but she needed to hear it.

"Hanging on to the best thing that's ever happened to me." He pushed away from the wall and stepped toward her, so close she could feel the heat from his body and hear his heart beating in her ears. "The most important thing. You can't leave me."

"I'm not the one leaving. You are. Aren't you?"

"If you think you're getting rid of me that easy, you'd better think again. I'm not going anywhere."

Joy erupted inside her. "But what about your charter business?"

"It's not the flying I like. It's the engines. I like breaking things down and building them back up and getting my hands dirty. I can do that right here. There hasn't been a really good auto shop in town since old man Witherspoon died two years ago."

"So you're staying." She blinked as the enormity of his words hit her. "You're really staying."

"I can't leave." He cradled her face and smoothed his

thumbs across her trembling bottom lip. "I love you, Holly. I always have, I just couldn't see it. I've never been in love before. Hell, I've never felt anything even close to what I'm feeling now. I didn't have a clue what was happening to me. And then when I realized it was damned powerful, I was scared shitless. But I'm not half as scared of the way I feel as I am of losing you." He closed his eyes and anguish gripped his expression. "When I found the house empty and I thought you'd left for good..." He shook his head and stared deep into her eyes. "I hope you love me because I sure as hell don't think I can handle living without you."

"I might be able to fit you into my new bathroom, if you're only packing one can of shaving cream."

"Are you saying what I think you're saying?" Hope fired in his gaze.

"If you think I'm saying that I love you and want to be with you, I am." When he started to slide his arms around her, she held him off. "But I still want a real relationship." She swallowed and forced herself to finish her ultimatum. "I want love *and* marriage." She swallowed and gathered her courage. "I want it all—a real home and a real family—or nothing at all."

He grinned and the tight coil in her chest started to unwind. "Does that mean you're asking me to marry you?"

"I'm asking when you're going to get around to doing the asking."

His expression faded and a serious light filled his eyes. "Will you marry me and live with me and make lots of babies with me?"

"Yes," she murmured, "and yes, and maybe."

"Maybe?"

"It depends on what you mean by 'lots.' If you're talking three or four, yes. If you mean seven or eight, we still have some talking to do. I've still got a lot of Ultimate Orgasms ahead of me, you know."

"Damned straight, you do," he vowed. "And a few of them might even be the edible variety." He drew her into his arms and hugged her fiercely. "I won't lose you. Not now. Not ever."

She slid her arms around him and held tight, her heart swelling with emotion and the certainty that he loved her as much as she loved him.

It was then that Holly realized she'd finally found what she'd been looking for her entire life, and it had nothing to do with four walls or a *Home Sweet Home* quilt sitting in the living room. It was about feeling good and comfortable and truly *belonging* somewhere.

Home, it seemed, was right there in Josh McGraw's strong arms.

* * * * *

*With Josh McGraw spoken for, the single girls
of Romeo have one less available bachelor
to chase. That is, until they realize that
Mason McGraw has come home.
The hunky rodeo cowboy is every bit as sexy as his
brother—and just as hard to tame....
Check out the fireworks in Blaze #198
TEXAS FIRE
by Kimberly Raye
August 2005
Here's a sneak peek....*

1

CHARLENE SINGER stood near the rear exit of the Elk's Lodge, stared at the man leaning against the bumper of the black four-by-four pickup truck directly in her line of escape and wished with all of her heart that she believed in alien abductions.

She needed a quick escape.

Her day—okay, make that her *month*—was quickly going from bad to worse. It had started when the queen of the gourmet sex desserts had moved to town and started poisoning the good women of Romeo with the insane theory that the way to a man's heart was through his senses. To add insult to injury, the women actually *believed* such nonsense. Ms. Sweet & Sinful had just preached to a lodge of Juliets—Romeo's local women's club—and had received a standing ovation. The Juliets had practically fallen over themselves to get to the table of handouts detailing several explicit recipes for sexual success. Feed him this and tease him with that, and he'll fall hook, line and sinker.

Yeah, right.

Charlene folded the tip sheet she'd swiped and stuffed it into the pocket of her slim-fit beige skirt. The

Juliets had been too enthralled by the advice to notice that Dr. Charlene Singer had actually attended one of their self-help luncheons. Talk about fuel for gossip during tomorrow's lunch rush down at the diner.

Romeo was the typical small Texas town. And like any typical small Texas town diner, the Fat Cow Café had become notorious for its platter-size chicken-fried steak smothered in cream gravy, served up with a generous side of homemade mashed potatoes and a great big scoop of "Didya hear? Willie McIntyre got caught wearing his wife's panty hose...."

The Juliets were already questioning Charlene's doctrine. The last thing she needed was for someone to get the idea that she'd jumped ship and was now anxious to try out Ms. Sweet & Sinful's recipes herself.

She'd come strictly to size up the competition, and now she intended to make a nice, clean getaway before the meeting officially adjourned and someone singled her out.

Fat chance with her only available getaway vehicle— a beige Lexus she'd bought last year—parked several feet away. On the opposite side of the man and the truck.

From bad to worse to disastrous.

Charlene closed her eyes and fought down a wave of panic. There were only three things in life that made her truly miserable—chocolate, *The Bachelor* and Mason McGraw.

It wasn't the sweet, rich taste that put everything dark, delicious and sinful at the top of her "unbearable things" list. She'd come closer to an orgasm with a bottle of Yoo-hoo and a box of truffles than with most of the men she'd dated. It was the dreadful "morning after," as in zits, as in a face covered in them that lasted longer than the dehydrated macaroni and cheese her father had kept in their weather emergency kit, along with batteries, bottled water and multiple cans of Spam.

The Bachelor ranked in the top three because of its blatant objectification of women. Sure, there was a lot of blah-blah on the man's part about finding a soul mate with brains and ambition, and Charlene supposed there could be a thread of truth to it. What guy wanted to spend till death do us part with a dumb, unambitious woman? But it wasn't an issue that any of the bachelors had to address. Thanks to the show's casting manager, said brains and ambition came wrapped in a drop-dead gorgeous body, preferably with perky breasts, blond hair and a laser-bleached smile. So much for *reality* TV.

As for number three on the list...

Her gaze slid to the hot body in question. He'd obviously not heard the rear exit door creak open because his attention remained fixed on the front entrance. An all-important fact which allowed her a few blessed moments to breathe, plan and study his profile.

Okay, so forget the breathing and planning. Mason McGraw had been back in Romeo all of two weeks and this was her first up-close look at him.

He wore faded Wrangler jeans that molded to his long, lean legs and cupped his tush which rested on the front bumper of the jacked-up truck. Scuffed, tan Ropers hooked at the ankles, the toes scarred and worn from climbing into one too many saddles. His back rested against the massive silver grill, his arms folded.

His biceps bulged, stretching the sleeves of his white T-shirt into a tight second skin. A beat-up straw Resistol sat low on his forehead. The brim curled down in the front and shielded his eyes from the blistering noon sun, the straw edges ragged from years of handling. Dark hair curled out from under his hat and brushed the collar of his cotton T-shirt. The faintest hint of stubble darkened his strong jaw and circled his sensuous mouth. His Adam's apple bobbed and the muscles in his jaw tensed as he chewed at a piece of straw that hung from the corner of his mouth.

Dark, delicious and sinful... Check!

Mason still looked as tempting as the most decadent piece of Godiva, which wasn't the problem in and of itself. She'd eyeballed many a good-looking man. But he wasn't just handsome. He had this peel-off-your-clothes grin that made women want to strip now and think later—much later—and Charlene was no exception.

Not that she would sink so low as to hook up with a man who'd made no secret that he liked his women beautiful and dumb. But seeing that grin full-on... Well, it made her at least contemplate the notion for a full five seconds before coming to her senses and realizing that this was the same guy who'd paid a quarter back in the sixth grade to see Joni Lynn Fuller's underpants.

Objectifies women... Check!

It hadn't mattered that Joni had been as intelligent as a bag of rocks, and about as sensitive. She'd had a pretty face to go with her pretty pink *Charlie's Angels* panties, and so Mason had been the first in line when

Joni had stepped into the closet to give sneak peeks at Sandra Huckaby's first girl/boy party.

Meanwhile, Charlene had stood as far away as possible, not the least bit anxious to have anyone see the white cotton *Hee-Haw* briefs her mom had bought on clearance at the local Kmart.

As if any of the boys would have given even a nickel for that.

Charlene hadn't been one of the cool girls with their lip gloss and Calvin Klein jeans. Rather, she'd been the tallest girl in the class, and the most awkward. Her jeans—whatever brand that happened to be on sale at Sears or Montgomery Wards—had always been an inch too short for her body. Her one attempt at a tube of Lip Smackers had created enough of a glare—can you say Mick Jagger lips?—to temporarily blind the captain of the basketball team and screw up a winning three pointer during the semifinals. At least that's what Sandra and Joni and the other "coolies" had said. To make matters worse, Charlene had worn thick glasses and battled monumental zits.

The only reason she'd even been invited to Sandra's party had been because their mothers had played in the same bridge club. A humiliation in and of itself. Unfortunately, it had only been the first of many that night. Before the evening had ended, she'd become known to every kid at Romeo Junior High as Charlie Horse Underpants.

Hey, there, Charlie Horse Underpants!
Here comes Charlie Horse Underpants!
How's it going, Charlie Horse Underpants?
The memories echoed in her head and her throat

tightened. The name didn't matter anymore. And it certainly didn't matter that Bobby Winchell down at the local Stop-n-Shop still said, "Well, well, if it ain't Charlie Horse Underpants," every time she stopped off for a loaf of bread or a six-pack of Diet Coke.

Despite that some immature people still felt the need to tease her, she wasn't about to burst into tears anymore. She was all grown up now and she realized that it wasn't about how a woman looked or what she wore that attracted a member of the opposite sex. It was her inner being. Her personality.

Be yourself and men—the reliable, till-death-do-us-part, potential soul mate kind, that is—will flock to you.

That was her motto now, one she preached with complete conviction not only in her private practice as a relationship therapist, but also twice a week at nearby Texas A & M to an auditorium full of enthusiastic sociology majors. *Forget the Boobs and Hair, It's All About Going Bare* had become the college's most popular course, and had earned Charlene tenure just this past year.

Tenure, she reminded herself. When most of the other professors her age were still working on thesis papers and building their credentials.

Charlene had already proven herself.

And her theory?

She ignored the question, steeled herself and stepped forward. It wasn't like she had to actually walk in front of him. She could go around the rear. But first, she had to clear several yards of open space without making any—

Crunchhh!

The sole of her Prada pump sank into the gravel and her breath caught.

Metal groaned and creaked. The pickup bobbed. More gravel crunched and crackled—sounds that had nothing to do with the tasteful, beige pumps she'd paid an obscene amount of money for during last month's shopping spree, and everything to do with worn boots and strong purposeful footsteps.

"Charlie?" The deep voice slid into her ears and sent a burst of heat through her.

Or maybe it was the sudden memory of her most embarrassing moment that did that.

Either way, she stiffened. Her head snapped to the side and she found herself staring into Mason's deep green eyes just the way she had that night when she'd accidentally left the bathroom door unlocked and he'd walked in on her. He'd had three boys trailing him and they'd all gotten a glimpse of her with her *Hee-Haw* panties down around her ankles.

But Mason had gotten the first look. The longest look. Before the other boys had started laughing and calling her the name that would follow her all the way to her high school graduation and beyond.

"*I see Paris, I see France. I see Charlie Horse Underpants!*"

"Well, well, if it isn't Charlie—"

"I'm not wearing any underpants," she blurted before he could say the rest of the dreaded name. "I mean, I *am* wearing underpants, but they're not the *Hee-Haw* ones. I don't wear those anymore. I wouldn't have worn them *ever*, except my mother had this thing for buying on sale and I didn't exactly have a choice. But now I buy my own underwear and I usually stick to solid colors. No horses. Not that the *Hee-Haw* ones even had horses. Technically, they were donkeys, but I guess Charlie Donkey didn't have the same ring to it."

Surprise registered in his dark green gaze. He tipped the brim of his hat back, as if to get a better look. "That's good to know," he said. And then he smiled.

No, forget the smile.

He *grinned,* his lips curving in that slow, sexy tilt that had made him the most sought-after boy in Romeo despite the fact that he had two almost identical brothers just as wild and wicked and handsome.

She wasn't sure what she'd expected, but it certainly wasn't the deep, husky, "I'm a plaid man myself."

The statement cut through her line of defense like a hot knife through butter and stirred an image of him wearing nothing but a pair of plaid boxers and a smile. Her mouth went dry and she licked her lips. "Well, I do have a pair with tiny hearts on them."

His grin widened. "Hearts are good."

Excitement rushed through her. A crazy reaction considering she couldn't care less what he thought. She hadn't bought the hearts for him, or any man for that matter. She'd bought them because they hadn't had any solids in her size and cut and she'd simply felt like splurging. A compulsion that had grown out of years of watching her mother budget and save and buy only marked-down merchandise.

She couldn't care less what he thought about her undies.

So why are you telling him?

To set the record straight. Because she'd endured too many names all these years and she'd never once fought back. She'd never really had the courage. Until Mason McGraw had been about to say the hated name and she'd had to stop him.

That, and because she was having a major brain fart thanks to the legendary grin.

"I have a master's in behavioral science," she heard herself say. Okay, she was still blurting unsolicited information, but at least it had nothing to do with her underwear. "I teach a class at A & M on female empowerment. I'm also a licensed relationship therapist. I have my own practice over near the courthouse."

"The white two-story colonial with the picket fence?" At her nod, he added, "Isn't that Dr. Connally's place?"

"I share the building with Stewart." That wasn't all she shared with him.

Oddly enough, her lips seemed to tighten around that last bit of information.

"We're dating," she finally managed. "We've been dating for nearly two years."

Josh let loose a low whistle. "Sounds serious."

"It is. I mean, I think it is. He hasn't proposed or anything, but I'm sure that's just a matter of time. We've known each other since we were kids. We're soul mates."

"Congratulations," he said. Oddly enough, the sentiment didn't seem to touch his gaze. "Is that the Connally guy from sophomore chemistry? The one who burned his eyebrows off with the Bunsen burner?"

"They finally grew back." After several special hair treatments in Austin. "You can't even tell now."

"Good for him."

"So what about you? What have you been up to?"

"I've been running my own ranch management consulting group, doing independent projects here and there. But now I'm home to run things at the Iron Horse."

"What about your business?"

"The Iron Horse is my business now."

Say goodbye, a voice whispered. *You've cleared the air, killed the teasing and done the proverbial small talk. Just excuse yourself, get into your car and leave.*

The sound of laughter drifted from the lodge entrance, signaling the dismissal of the meeting. Any minute, the doors would bust open and she'd be busted.

"Married?" she heard herself ask.

"Are you kidding?"

"Fiancée?"

"Hardly."

"Significant other?"

"Only a horse named Winston."

She tried to resist the smile tugging at her lips. "So what are you doing here? At the lodge?"

"Josh is inside proposing right now, so I thought I'd give him a little moral support."

"Really? I could have sworn five seconds ago that just the thought gave you the heebie-jeebies."

"Actually, it does. And it used to have the same effect on my brother. Until he met this woman." He shrugged and glanced behind him at the entrance, a puzzled look on his face. As if Josh were about to cut off his arm rather than pledge his life to that special woman.

"What's her name?"

"Holly Farraday," he said as his gaze collided with Charlene's. "She makes desserts or something."

"Ultimate Orgasms," Charlene clarified. "And Cherry Body Bon Bons and Daring Divinity, and a dozen other things with suggestive names."

His eyebrows kicked up a notch. "Come again?"

"She makes aphrodisiac desserts that supposedly entice the senses and put a person in 'the mood.'"

Amusement glittered in his gaze. "Must be some damned powerful desserts."

"It's all propaganda to sell her product. Attraction doesn't lie in the five senses. It goes deeper than that."

He eyed her. "Is that how it is with you and Dr. Steven?"

"His name's Stewart, and that's exactly how it is. He doesn't need me flitting around, half-dressed, serving him glorified chocolate cake to make him feel frisky. Just talking with me is enough for that."

His gaze swept from her head to her toes and back up again as he seemed to think on the matter. He finally shrugged. "So why are you here?"

"Research purposes."

He arched an eyebrow before giving her another grin. "That's what they all say, sugar."

Her stomach fluttered and she stiffened. "I have to know what bunk is circulating in order to effectively debunk it. I'm sure her desserts are delicious, but there's no way merely eating one can heighten the attraction between two people."

He gave her a wink. "Depends how you eat it."

The gleam in his eyes told her he wasn't talking about using plates or forks. Something sharp and sweet tickled between her legs and her breath caught.

"I…" She licked her lips and instantly regretted it when his gaze hooked on her mouth. Desire brightened his eyes.

Desire?

Because of some simple lip-licking?

Maybe on the most superficial level.

But Charlene didn't advocate superficial. She preached depth and commitment and destiny.

"Here's my card," she told him, eager to shatter the strange spell that had suddenly surrounded her. She pulled the familiar piece of vellum from the inside pocket of her blazer and handed it to him.

"Excuse me?"

"In case you ever need any therapy."

She saw the twinkle in his gaze and she braced herself for the grin she knew would follow.

"Well, lookee what the cat dragged in." Lolly Mae Langtree's voice killed his expression and drew his attention.

A mix of relief and dread rolled through Charlene as she turned to see the blond, blue-eyed, once-upon-a-time captain of the Romeo cheerleading squad standing in the open double doorway.

"I was just—" Charlene started, but Lolly cut her off.

"If it isn't Mason McGraw," the woman declared as she stepped forward. She didn't so much as spare Charlene a glance. "I'd heard you were back, but it's high time I saw for myself."

"Mason McGraw!" another voice shrieked as the double doors opened again and several more women spilled out into the parking lot.

"Talk about a surprise!" said another.

"What a sight for sore eyes."

"You're looking as good as ever!"

Charlene quickly found herself pushed aside as the women surrounded Mason.

She ignored the strange tightening in her chest. It wasn't as if Mason's throng of adoring fans actually bothered her. She would have to be attracted to him for that, which she most certainly wasn't.

It took more than a great face and a hot body and a few suggestive remarks to seduce Dr. Charlene Singer. She looked for substance when it came to men, and so an attractive—a very attractive—package was irrelevant.

She turned on her heel and headed for her car. Better to forget Mason McGraw wrapped up in his cotton T-shirt and skintight Wranglers.

Better, but not easy, she realized as she caught herself chancing a glance behind her.

Not by a long shot.

COMING NEXT MONTH

#195 WHO'S ON TOP? Karen Kendall
The Man-Handlers, Bk. 1

In this battle between the sexes, they're both determined to win. Jane O'Toole is supposed to be assessing Dominic Sayers's work-related issues, but the sexual offers he delivers make it hard to stay focused. But once they hit the sheets, the real challenge is to see who's the most satisfied...

#196 THE MORNING AFTER Dorie Graham
Sexual Healing, Bk. 1

Not only did he stay until morning, he came back! Nikki McClellan can heal men through sex. And her so-called gift is powerful enough that a single time is all they need. At this rate she's destined to be a one-night wonder...until Dylan Cain. Which is a good thing, because he's so hot, she doesn't want to let him go!

#197 KISS & MAKEUP Alison Kent
Do Not Disturb, Bk. 3

Bartender Shandi Fossey is mixing cool cocktails temporarily at Hush—the hottest hotel in Manhattan. So what's a girl to do when sexy Quentin Marks offers to buy *her* a drink? The famous music producer can open a lot of doors for her—but all she really wants is to enter the door leading to his suite....

#198 TEXAS FIRE Kimberly Raye

Sociology professor Charlene Singer has always believed that it's what's on the outside that counts. That's got her...nowhere. So she's going to change her image and see if she gets any luckier. Only, she soon realizes she'll need more than luck to handle rodeo cowboy Mason McGraw....

#199 U.S. MALE Kristin Hardy
Sealed with a Kiss, Bk. 2

Joss Chastain has a taste for revenge. Her family's stamps worth $4.5 million have been stolen, and Joss will stop at nothing to get them back, even if it means seducing private eye John "Bax" Baxter into helping her. As tensions rise and the chemistry ignites, Joss and Bax must risk everything to outsmart the criminal mastermind...and stay alive.

#200 WHY NOT TONIGHT? Jacquie D'Alessandro
24 Hours: Blackout, Bk. 2

When Adam Clayton fills in at his friend's photography studio, he never dreamed he'd be taking *boudoir photos*—of his old flame! Too bad Mallory *has* a boyfriend—or, at least she *did* before she caught him cheating. She's not heartbroken, but she is angry. Lucky for Adam, a blackout gives him a chance to make her forget anyone but him...

www.eHarlequin.com

HBCNM0705